AI … BER

NOV…

SERIES ONE

GRIFFIN TERMINAL

ALWAYSEPTEMBER

Published by Konaga Publishing Lancashire UK

Contact: info@alwayseptember.com

Website: www.alwayseptember.com

Cover Art: konaga.co.uk

Character Art: konaga.co.uk

Merchandise: konaga.store

ISBN: 978-1-3999-8152-1 [eBook]
ISBN: 978-1-3999-9093-6 [PrintBook]

TRILOGY

KONRAD MCLEAN

BOOK ONE
GRIFFIN TERMINAL

BOOK TWO
ETHEREAL SOULS

BOOK THREE
THE LIONS GATE

www.alwayseptember.com

FOREWORD

On many occasions I often wondered what happens to the knowledge gained through our earth experiences, an elusive quest maybe, just like imagining the end of the great void as we look skyward. Eternity seems to be built into our minds, and although fictional this story is, the concept of spirit reincarnation permeates numerous historical texts, human belief systems, and recounted experiences that touch upon the realm beyond. After years of observing the intricate network of animated organisms, working in symbiotic connection, coexisting and deriving mutual benefits, from the towering trees to the imperceptible microorganisms - there arises the notion that maybe the harmonious union might embody a prevailing consciousness. A realisation that we are tethered to the same linked chain, separated by our language and understanding that enables us to enjoy our journey, here for purpose to expand ourselves and enrich others. This realisation brought to my attention the interconnectedness of all things. I must maintain an open radio signal, fine-tune my modulation, and ultimately broadcast my thoughts.

I hope you enjoy this story

CONTENTS

THE CREATOR

SAMUAL ALDERMAN

After decades of keeping the families secret, the dark days had come to pass. The final chapter of Samual Alderman's life had left an indelible mark of mystery to be solved. His graceful charm embrued a sophisticated mind of reality, an understanding of problems at source, and the answers. After reaching his 52nd year, disenchanted of nobility and reverence, he pursued the dark riddle that his father never finished. That is, the sourcing and trapping of the human soul. While long considered an unfathomable enquiry, soon this became known as soul spanning. An altered state of life as an outcome, a living soul inside another physical host.

After a lengthy road of invention, finally around 1753, the mind was accessed, entered into by another sentient being. A new end to contemporary science, and from here began The Entanglement. In a life where thoughts remain hidden and the only restriction to voyage are your eyes, seekers like Alderman ventured beyond the senses into a world of electric dreams, thereby discovering the Lions Gate, starting a quest for the key to that gate. Maybe the saviour to mankind's most elusive and frightening question. Death.

- K.S. Granger
June 1788

LANGTON LODGE

Upon the hill facing the ridge that's where it was. A tall shadow, always dark, even when the clouds would give way to moonshine, you needed good eyes or it would just disappear into the woodland. We had a meadow not so far away, but I only venture out, you know, within the barn and the boathouse. It always was slow the pace of life, until after that winter broke, the mist was there then. Guess you could have called it a challenge to say the least, but doing what I could to help, this time I called it in. Suppose when you're running scared of something, there ain't no time to ask yourself what's happening.

We gamed a stare to an understanding nod. Making a note in my book and smoothing the ridge of my hat. “Okay that will be all for today Mr Robert’s.”

A deep rumble choked the clouds. Our attention momentarily skyward then back to a brewing face off. A stunted twig turning at his mouths edge served to frame my exit.

“The wind . . . it’s always gonna change direction, we're lucky we have the sun for consistency. I do understand these events date back many years, Mr Roberts . . . just one more thing. The boathouse light, do you always keep it on late at night?”

“If you weren’t there Mr Kessler, how would y’know if I left the light on?”

“Well . . . I took a look around and, noticed it’s independent to the house. Also Miss Tyler said the light was on at about 11pm.” With persistent stubbornness Robert’s responded with baited breath.

“I only leave it on when I’m a fishing. Maybe Miss Tyler saw some reflection on the lake. Fireflies are in season too . . . they light up just about everything.”

We eyeballed another stare amidst the windy rustle of the trees.

“You’re not incorrect about the possibility Mr Roberts. Okay, we are done here.”

He was an awkward character Robert's, darkly transparent, couldn't quite put my finger on what made me off-kilter. Maybe his braced overalls or rough bearded complexion . . . a nudge told me it wasn't stacking up. He couldn't have made those things happen, he hasn't got the know-how. As the rain beat the ground for the third day, the river running through the nearby town of Hamilton became swollen and the local people knew the danger ahead if there wasn't a shift in the clouds. The grey steel look on the faces as I drove through shifted my decision on renting a room until Friday. The day was Wednesday the eighth of September.

Even though early afternoon, it resembled a sunless winter night. The lush green forests were transitioning into vibrant hues of fiery red and orange, marking the arrival of another season of the fall. I headed for a place out of town called Langton Lodge, about a thirty minute drive away after seeing an ad in the diner. Heavy rain pelted the windscreen, visibility was poor, and the road transformed into a dirt track. A short time passed and the dark thick forest opened up to a stone and cedar wood lodge standing alone. Smoke bellowed out of the chimney stacks and the surrounding grounds were neat, procured.

Parking the brake on my Ford next to a green Buick and what looked like a cream Hudson, I opened the door to angry storm clouds, grabbing my bag for the dash towards the steps. Shaking the drops off under the canopy, the dimly lit porch entrance led to twin doors sided with glass. On the push the bell rang to a shingaling, revealing a panelled hallway offering a glimpse of a grand staircase at the back. My leather shoes echoed on the maple floor as the corridor opened into a dark spacious room filled with a collection of books standing floor to ceiling. The vivid colours danced to the flames of a grand wood burning fire. A counter desk next to the staircase, behind a man seated, looking up breaking a smile so I politely lifted my hat.

"Hello there." Making his way around the desk I waited on the first move, the customs can be finicky in remote areas. Stepping closer, he'd be around six feet in height, neat with round spectacles, gracefully aged.

"I guess you need a room?"

"Yes, maybe for a couple of nights. The best room, I don't mind paying."

He gestured with his arm to the left. "Please, hang your wet jacket at the end of the rack. The standards are high, however, my room isn't for rent." Moving towards the orange flames of the open fire he clasped a brass hamlet from the stone surround, placing his foot on the hearth.

"Will you be requiring electricity?"

"Why of course." Placing my shoulder bag on the wood floor, hanging my jacket and hat, I noticed the rack wasn't empty. He shouldered the brass poker and began charming the logs.

"I was referring to electrical items, like a shaver maybe. We have shortages because our guest in room twelve works day and night."

What kind of work I wondered as I stepped down into the living quarters to survey the library of books, hundreds upon hundreds.

"By the way my names Mr Kessler. Daniel Kessler . . . and you are?"

"Mr Kristof . . . your host, Michael Kristof. You must be cold, please be seated. Cloak yourself in nature's greatest gift."

The welcoming heat radiated my cheeks. I reclined on the buttoned back leather chair to dry my bones. The wood chipped and split with another poker roll, returning the hamlet, he relaxed in the seat opposite. A sophisticated look, a well-dressed man.

"Do you retain many guests out here in the sticks Mr Kristof?"

"If you mean keeping a record of entries into this establishment then you are correct Mr Kessler. We are always curious of our guests. Sometimes though, the curious can make home to assumptions."

"Well, I like to render my curiosity and think of it as a blessing. I was wondering . . . why have you such a large collection of books?"

"Well . . . you could say they are not mine."

"I assumed you are the owner of the establishment?" Ringing his hands he hinted a grin.

"Yes you are correct. However, the books you observe are thoughts and writings of other people." As the clock ticked away on the side table, the heavy rains lashed the Lodge windows to the rear. Crouching forward he spoke with dubious eyes. "Are you well read Mr Kessler?"

"I prefer practical applications of my skills but yes, I've covered some reading ground, albeit more factual writings. If you are referring to fiction then no, that isn't my strong suit."

"That is a shame. The fiction Mr Kessler. An improvising of the mind while never sharing in the same visions of another reader. Maybe storytelling isn't your line of work then?"

Neatening my collar with a sense of reservation while he surveyed the flames. "Are you talking about the imagination?"

"Yes, the imagination Mr Kessler. A sixth sense, an implicit function or the minds eye as they say."

Just a hunch, I don't wanna get tied into obscure ideologies and lose my focus. I'm miles from nowhere and there are many pending questions. The random lightening flash etched eerie shadows of trees onto the library walls. Feeling a nudge of uneasiness, I took a stand and had a mooch around. With just the fire crackle and the ticking of the clock you could count the leather strides I made. Intrigued by the colours and sheer volume of books I edged closer, peering at the titles on the spines.

"A question if I may Mr Kessler?" He insisted.

"Fire away, anytime." I quipped.

"When you sleep within the darkness and your visions are clear, vivid. Would you conclude this was your mind's eye?"

"I often dream in the darkness if that is your question. However, I also do a lot of daydreaming. How do you account for that Mr Kristof?"

The clock chimed and chimed again on the hour of three. Yet, the third strike didn't arrive. We both stared to the marble table where it sat. A classical look, a black ebony finish, gold catchments and ring face. There were several decorated clocks in the room but appear muted.

"I never took you as a daydreamer Mr Kessler. Your position as the enquirer I do respect. Dreams do infer that you are somehow in a sub-conscious state of mind. However, I believe consciousness is prevailing throughout the day and night."

"I'm mindful during the day and at night if that's what you mean?" Grabbing a book from the shelving it was malleable on touch, weird. The characters inside seemed to be scrambled into a codex with blank pages towards the end.

"Maybe life could be represented just like the spine of that book you hold Mr Kessler; the prologue, the body and the epilogue. Or your past, your presence and your future."

Sliding the book back into the casing I ran my fingers over some other spines, many without titles. "Yes I can see your analogy Mr Kristof. Life could be viewed in those three stages. I'd be inclined to agree. Also . . . nobody would say that you were unconscious when sleeping." Stepping back towards the fire, the wood panelling reflecting the shimmer of the flame, I sided with the leather chair. I needed answers for these strange happenings. He must know something.

"May I ask of you myself now Mr Kristof?"

A silent nod, his hands clasped as the fires choked a crackle accompanied by the rains ever present chatter.

"How many years have you held residency in these parts?"

"My time here has been pleasant, full of many gates. Some for the better and some for the worse. About 24 years at this proprietary and 35 years in residence. I'd say since around 1897."

"Don't you mean doors, Mr Kristof."

"Certainly not, I mean gates Mr Kessler." Implicit in his meaning I guessed on first glance, detail was his.

"What do you know about the mine incident or the animals running off the cliff face freakishly last weekend?" I carefully gauged his reaction. Unperturbed, he continued in an elegant tone.

"Yes, the mine was an awful disaster and so too the cattle. Some of the villagers think it's poor maintenance structurally . . . what do you think . . . Detective?" Reclining on a shrewd smile with both hands wreathed, the cynical stare behind his spectacles reflecting the fire caught me unaware. No doubt he would have perceived my change of countenance, the dynamic shifting.

"Assuming that I work for the state Mr Kristof, let us continue. It sounds like you are friendly with the villagers ... so what about the swine?" His response hesitant, a composure intact in his eccentric stare.

"They were chased over the edge. A simple conclusion."

"Several miles they were from their hog owners field."

"Are you a hog farmer by trade Mr Kessler?"

"I know hogs don't do cross country Mr Kristof. There were 40 counted in the cliffs. No vehicle tracks or footprints."

"A very unsightly death I'm sure. However, solving animal crime might not be your forte." Calmly standing and leaning towards the fire, he rattled the brass poker and began shunting the wood embers up the large stone stack. "If they were not chased, then they possibly heard a sound? Whatever they were running from, it seems fright might play a part."

"Maybe. There are only a few conclusions to be drawn. Tell me, do you know of any military testing facilities in this part of Michigan?"

"Working for the government I would have thought that would be my question to you Mr Kessler?"

He's a guarded pundit for sure, well seasoned. It's gonna be a long simmer to the surface. His head shifted, awaiting my response. "I'm the best part of a country away from the usual territory I operate. As for yourself Mr Kristof, you are a long-standing inhabitant of the area. Where would your nose lead you about the mysterious events over the previous years?"

Another prod of the timbers coaxed a brighter flame. He then clanged the hamlet against the brass rail, resting it at the fireside. Reclining opposite and intertwining his fingers while breathing a sigh to raised cheeks.

"My dear Mr Kessler. Your nose will only lead you to your conclusion and so too will mine. Each a personal vision, in our imagination, painted pictures of the mind. Your work revolves around death, building a story back to a reasonable conclusion does it not? Yet death itself . . . is it not something you have questioned?"

"I tend to focus on the living. Do I ever ask about death as the end? Well it's not something I question, only the events leading up to the finish line."

"Is that your modus operandi?" His eyebrows raised. "The tall and short, there is no more?"

"I'm afraid that's all Mr Kristof. I tend to focus on one case at a time. Considering my position, I'm more interested in you . . . than you are of me." It was my turn to break a rye smile on the turning of the shoe. "I wouldn't want to implicate you as a suspect Mr Kristof. Although necessity has requirements, after all it is a living case with possible dead members. You have no doubt become aware of the happenings around these parts. Tell me, the mine incident, it is understood there was copper being extracted and smelted in the town. I observed the sales ledger at the smelting house and recall seeing Langton Estates Incorporated. Is this your business?"

The front door swung open as the bell resonated loudly accompanied by a gust of wind and rain sweeping the corridor. In walked an elegant woman in her thirties wearing a long coat and heels. The host Mr Kristof fawned a large grin, evidently recognising her.

"Good afternoon Miss Biedermann. Let me take your overcoat. Please allow me to introduce an inquisitive visitor. Mr Dan Kessler."

"Hello Mr Kessler. I'm Amelia . . . Amelia Biedermann."

"A pleasure to meet you Miss Biedermann. I assume you are already a guest at the Lodge?"

"Correct. Please, make use of the drinks cabinet. Over near the couch." Pointing with her manicured hands. "Make it a red wine, any will suffice. A hot water if I may Mr Kristof, thank you. The endless rain can have an inimical effect on you." Addressing her long dark hair in the mirror aside the coat rack she stepped down towards the fire, gracefully making herself neat. I handed her a glass of red while Mr Kristof was in the kitchen.

"I assume such an attractive woman has a fiancé?"

"That is a private matter if you are coursing for a back story. Please forgive my rude abruptness Mister . . ."

"Kessler . . . Dan Kessler. Please, let me take your jacket?" I took a pace forward and her tone changed.

"No, that will be fine." Stopping me in my tracks, we exchanged a cold glance as I became seated.

"Here you are, the water you asked for. Your mail from Tuesday."

"Thank you Mr Kristof. Have you invited Mr Kessler over, or is he a new guest?" Her accent seeded a memory, reminiscent of someone.

"He will be staying a few nights. He visited out of the blue isn't that correct Mr Kessler?" I flickered a smile as Kristof sarcastically quipped. "It is not often we have a detective staying. The one who keeps seeking more doors."

I felt isolated for a brief moment. Miss Biedermann's arms were stretched out, her hands upright clasping the heat beside the fire.

"Do you play chess Mr Kessler?"

"Yes I do. Maybe another time we can game? Several incidents have occurred around this district and I was chatting to Mr Kristof about the mine accident. Did you hear?"

"The copper mine?" she responded.

"Yes . . . how do you know they extract copper?"

"I thought it was copper. I could be wrong, is this a detective game Mr Kessler. Why then you caught me out!" We coupled a relaxing grin.

"Your humour is a refreshing change Miss Biedermann." I sarcastically quipped glancing to Kristof. "I do apologise for being abrupt, let us take our time." Signalling to the chair opposite. "If we could, a brief conversation."

Kristof waltzed to the tall windows, meandering near the large desk, his eyes toward the storm clouds. Miss Biedermann adjusted her dress, sipping the hot water while taking the chair. Her scented fragrance touched my nose, curating another memory.

"You seem quite comfortable Mr Kessler. Have you visited before?"

"Maybe your perfumed scent reminded me of something. Just so you know, it is my first time in Michigan." Her focus switched to my hand.

"I notice no wedding band. It must be a lonely life your work?"

"Well it seems we have something in common Miss Biedermann." We chuckled as she swapped for the wine glass to her lips.

"May I ask . . . your residency here at Langton Lodge. Would you say frequent?"

"My current lodging is around three weeks. Travelling long distance makes this location ideal. I'd say a number of occasions over the years." Twisting in her chair to his shadowed figure. "What would you say Mr Kristof?"

Moving his head to the side, arms behind his back. "Maybe in excess of four occasions, some short . . . some long." I had a fleeting thought - maybe they were in cahoots?

"Tell me please, are you here on business?"

"Yes. I work for a quarry merchants about 300 miles down state. We have a shared quarry over the hills near here. Do you mind Mr Kessler?" Holding the large glass of red wine to her lips, she gave way to two large gulps, surprised, I simpered to a pause.

"I see . . . so what minerals are extracted from quarrying this region Miss Biedermann?"

"Well it changes, mineral to an ore, too location." Unfolding her legs and tabling the glass she pushed herself to stand, her hand running the back of the chair. "Many minerals have been found in this area so you could say it's a hotspot for enthusiastic entrepreneurs and miners. You can't get in the way of the hunt. The markets change for materials, supply and demand, all the usual cycles of events." Glancing back to the windows. "Is my room prepared Mr Kristof?"

"Yes, certainly. There is hot water for bathing."

I leaned forward in the chair. "Leaving so soon Miss Biedermann?"

"Yes, we have had a brief conversation. I need to bathe detective, my vitality has been consumed with travelling for hours since sunrise." She approached the staircase with her heel on the first step. "I will re-emerge this evening. Are you becoming a guest?"

"Yes, I think so. Tell me, the material mined from the quarries. What yields the more favourable income?" Maybe I can get an answer out of the day. They are such a strange combo.

"Copper. Copper is your answer. I will educate you later Mr Kessler. Take care of our guest Mr Kristof."

THE HOST

Miss Biedermann retreated to her room. Our engaging in rapport, yet brief, seemed to fuel Kristof's cagey aura. The ominous shadows flashed the room, the rain and windy howls and occasional thunderous groans compounded my isolation, an imbuing sense that I needed to stay focused. There are too many kooks around these parts and, although the company generous, stimulating, it appears to be cleverly evasive. As soon as the storm subsides I need to visit Miss Tyler about the boathouse to try and find . . . Kristof came back into earshot towards the fireplace.

"If you don't mind, the question earlier Mr Kristof. The sales ledger at the smelting house -

Langton Estates Incorporated. Is this your business?"

Slanting in the chair, his sharp leather shoe pointed towards me.

"Does my name appear on the shareholder documentation Mr Kessler? You cannot see the people involved in the sales ledger only the company and the sale item. I presume it was copper buying from the smelter in the town. Does that conclude your matter."

I need to change tact, he seems a step ahead. There's something perfidious about his elusive satire.

"I came across a few names you might know, Granger and Berwick. Any of those open a gate for you?"

Walking to the rear, rolling the calendar date on the desk to peer above his spectacles at me. He turned to observe the sky through the tall windows.

"I preferred Miss Biedermann's wit. No, neither names open any doors for me. What I do know is the name has drawn you here Mr Kessler. It is the beginning of the fall. The winds and clouds fighting to get their own way through the end of another season gone wild." Twisting his arm and viewing his watch, tapping on the face. "It is early but appears late with the storm clouds - would you care for a stiff drink Mr Kessler?"

"Yes. Maybe a brandy thanks."

Besides the reception desk were decanters and spirit glasses. Kristof took hold and began pouring then a heavy shunting noise from upstairs caught our attention.

"Don't be alarmed. It is just the comings and goings of guests. Why, somebody could have been seated in that very same spot as you are today Mr Kessler, and heard the same noise yesterday."

Passing the drink, the aroma of liquor flushed through my sinuses with the burn on my throat. He reclined across from me so I enquired of the somebody.

"Was that somebody a visitor or a guest?"

"What is the difference? They are all visitors and guests at the same time - you are a visitor that is becoming a guest. After your stay you might visit as a guest if I invite you back, then you will become my guest visitor. You see these are all endless beginnings. I'm not your host at the moment but soon will be, just like I am to several other guests."

Hmmm endless beginnings, exactly what Miss Tyler uttered. "Tell me, endless beginnings, is this local slang. A colloquialism around these parts?"

"Possibly. It is more of an understanding. Usually there is no energy after the finish line, the end, it's already spent. Why, you said it yourself, the events leading up to the finish are your focused pursuit. That is the natural course of any race Mr Kessler. Then . . . it begins again."

"I understand the energy is spent in ones life concludes, unfortunately in death. The race has finished. What are you implying Mr Kristof?"

Flushing another brandy, he opened a silver box to his right and offered a cigar with a high brow. Removing the seal, the flint from the lighter sparked the air as I inhaled the sweet dry taste of the leaf.

"Life's energy can resemble a race as a time stamp. Eternity seems to be built into us, the imaginary future as a narrative serves as our fuel, a prospector for the mind." Pausing and scooping his glass. "Thinking around the future, optimism must prevail. I suppose the word is tied to hope and faith. Unfortunately, you and I cannot be timeless keepers. You see Mr Kessler, forever is times presence that you respect mindfully, but as you move forward in the race, time shows no empathy to your physical host and concludes in death. An eventuality that seems such a waste of intellect. Your only restriction too longevity is the physical host you abide."

We both chewed some more tobacco while I pondered over his proverbial idioms. A blanket of smoke sat above our heads as my eyes continued to pierce his glass lenses.

"I'm a realist Mr Kristof. I do see death regularly, but are you suggesting there is a beginning at death? Is that the future you talk about?"

"Yes it well maybe. Our presence is controlled by something not of this world. The invisible, the ethereal. It in itself is an altered state. Like you and I, a physical entity coupled with an invisible entity. We are both spirits in a material world." The flames danced at the edges of his spectacles. "You see Mr Kessler, your dealings as a detective to date have been chasing the past physical host and yet, the controller of that host has already left the scene!"

Grinning he brushed his jacket lapel gazing into the flames. The light flickered again to silhouettes blanching the room. I sauntered over to the drinks table, peering down my shoulder for his notice. “Do you mind?” Another brandy warmly flushed through my cheeks as I held his thought, gently pacing back to my chair. “Your satire amuses me Mr Kristof. I suppose delivering the evidence that the controller did not die at the same time would prove difficult for you in a court of law.”

A chugging of the cigar belched another ring of smoke. Behind the cloud bore a cunning smile.

“Correct . . . The presence of law is essential just as order exists all around us. You can only police or govern the aspects you have written down. You’ve heard the saying the pen is mightier than the sword?” I nodded while folding my arms, pondering his theme. “We can only pen the future. However, any foretelling is never to be seen in the present, only after the event has taken place. Unless of course you were living in the future, then time has no bearing on you. Imagine the soul continually alive and spanning generations, a perpetual presence.” Sampling his glass he leant forward with a familiar solemn gaze. “Would you ever consider a journey into the future Mr Kessler?”

I phased out for a moment. I recall being asked the very same questions years ago. Somewhere in time the journey, the future in my memory . . . the uncomfortable delving into my belief and peering into my core fabric wasn't on my original agenda.

"Mr Kessler. Would you consider such a journey?"

Hesitant of his persistency, I inhaled a large drag of the cigar and blew the smoke in his direction. "Of course. I don't mind taking a chance. If you were to mention the unknown, then that's a whole new game. A strange proposition if that's what it is."

"It is for consideration, an enquiry to gauge your interest." With eyebrows raised I searched my thoughts and pondered out loud.

"The soul . . . hmmm. Maybe I could agree, it is an invisible entity. How can you be sure the soul and body are not tied together and death encapsulates both?"

The bell rang on reception, looked like No.7 on the painted plaque. Kristof began moving to the reception desk.

"Is everything ok?" I queried.

"Yes, business as usual."

Perusing the room, upon the glass table an ornate chess board with pieces in midst game. The red leather couches draped in animal fur made me wonder if the rooms were of equal comfort.

"Your welcome to more drink, also food can be arranged." Pointing to the rear windows where the rain was beating. "We have a library Mr Kessler, why not choose a book from the many, please be my guest. You will find the ladder that traverses the bookshelves, be careful with your step."

As he strode the staircase, I made my way to the rear of the Lodge. Heavy embroidered curtains and a burgundy valance covered the stone muntins. Mapping the desk we're charts that intrigued me. Number sequences that were not monetary figures, more like co-ordinates. I spent a few years in reconnaissance for the army in my early twenties, but they weren't, in fact, they didn't resemble anything I've seen before. Coded instructions maybe, a language of symbols. On my left another room, recessed with double doors, a step down and a walkway with an even larger collection of books and a piano. Above the door in carved wooden type 'The Perpetual Presence'. Before I could take my first step I felt the warmth of the sun on my back as dust became visible through straight rays into the room. Broken clouds yielded an opportunity to see Miss Tyler I thought. You gotta get your coat and go. I grabbed my hat and at the bottom of the staircase raised my voice.

"Mr Kristof, can you hear me?"

"Yes, Mr Kessler."

"I have to dash - hold onto the room, what number is it?"

"Number eight, top of the stairs to the right. Are you joining myself and Miss Biedermann this evening for dinner around six o'clock?"

"Yes, I will be here."

Another chime from the ebony clock, the hands were on the fourth hour. I paused at the second chime, staring to the mantle on the third, strangely the fourth never arrived. Rolling the jacket around my shoulders and grabbing my bag I exited, stepping down the wooden porch. Besides the large oak tree approaching the car, a light was shining from the outhouse. 'Not now' passed my thoughts, I gotta keep my pants dry over my shoes, Miss Tyler's home was no doubt well kept. The engine fired as I slowly traversed the potholes on the main road. I got within ten minutes from the destination and a man on a horse came into view. I slowed on him gesturing through the steamy glass then pulled over and moved the winder, squeaking the glass, he came into focus.

"How do." A deep tone he had, bearded, wearing a green poncho.

"I'm good thanks. What do I owe the pleasure?"

"There is a ford in the road ahead from the rainfall just so you know. You might need to detour, unless you have a horse?"

I smiled without showing my teeth. "Well then my friend, do you want to swap vehicles or, can you point me in the right direction? Much appreciated."

"Around 1000 yards, just after the water tower swing left. When you reach the old schoolhouse, take a right. That should get you back on track."

"Okay thanks."

Watching him disappear in my rear view mirror I was dubious about the advise. Sometimes though you gotta accept someones just helping out.

Approaching the water tower I swung left up a small track through thick woodland. Surfacing to large open fields, the sun began to break the clouds and vision was good. There it was, an abandoned schoolhouse. Gliding past the boarded up building after a curious stare I negotiated the isolated track to reach the bottom back onto the main drag. A few miles further and the road dipped beneath the land mass, rising to emerge into view the lakes clear blue waters through the forest. The sky still painted with daubs of grey, the road widened and Miss Tyler's residence appeared on the ridge. I headed through the walled gates labelled Oakland's Mount and up onto the private road. The house, impressive with pale blues and white wooden balcony surrounds got me pondering on the great views over the lake she must have. Stopping aside the turning circle outside the entrance, turning the engine key, my door thudded on the close. A maid appeared on hand to greet me.

"Hello, can I help?"

"I'm here to see Miss Tyler, she said to visit anytime. I'm Detective Kessler."

"Please, step inside detective."

I managed to have a brief discussion with Miss Tyler in the Hamilton department store that led to questioning Mr Roberts. The disappearance of two travellers on the lake prompted the visit. Their boat, nor their bodies have been found.

"Can I fix you a drink? A tea maybe?" Said the maid.

"Yes, tea no milk. One cube thanks."

"Please be seated. Miss Tyler will not be long."

As she entered the door to the kitchen I studied form. The white clinical rooms had very few textiles which surprised me for a lady's dwelling. Family memorabilia painted the walls, reminiscent of a dynastic family tree. Crouching to the detail of the sideboard trinkets, through the glass octopus I stopped at the groan of time resonating from the grandfather clock. Attentive to the swing of the pendulum, moving side to side, clicking and ticking. A fascinating device I thought.

"Your tea Mr Kessler." I jumped - the maid was stood by my side.

"My. You caught me off guard for a moment."

"So sorry to startle you detective. Please take a chair."

"Yes sure." The maid scuppered. To avoid anymore surprises I sunk my back deep into the green leather couch next to large windows overlooking the lake. A picturesque painting of tranquility.

"Hello Mr Kessler. What do I owe the pleasure?"

Wearing a head to toe sequinned dress with dark braided hair she was refined. No garb, only a watch under her left sleeve. I stood, hat in hand, waiting for her to be seated.

"Good day Miss Tyler. A brief visit to inquire about incidents around the area. I'm trying to connect the dots after our previous chat."

"Yes very well Mr Kessler. Did you know the other detective from your bureau. He arrived a few years ago?"

"I know of him Miss Tyler. He disappeared to my knowledge." She glanced towards the lake as I paused. "He was here regards the other incidents. Let's hope it's our last investigation."

"So tell me, what information are you seeking?"

Laying down my hat to the side and maintaining eye contact, I postured through the window towards the waters. "The men missing on the lake. They hired a boat from the Turnpike Depot near the railroad. Are you familiar with the place?"

Placing her hands together on her lap. "Well it has been in the family for years. The lake is two miles from tip to tip and the only place to hire boats is at the Depot. That is correct."

"I checked with . . . why, you will already be acquainted with Mr Duxbury, the manager of the Depot?"

"Yes of course Mr Kessler. He has held residency for over ten years."

Lifting the cup I tasted the tea, my head rolling forward. "He said that the men stole the boat. No signatures and no payment. Possibly around ten o'clock on the night."

"Yes I can validate Mr Duxbury's account." A sharp reply while she faced the window view. "If you mean why didn't we report the theft, well, we thought if it was a drunken reveller then the boat would be returned or found, and that would be the end of the matter."

Placing the tea cup down to a chink of the saucer I squinted my eyes towards the woodland. Clouds were casting shadows over the waters expanse in time to the pendulums swinging arm. She seemed abrupt and inconsiderate of the events, so I thought I'd remind her. "You do understand I'm here investigating the possible murder of the two men who hired the boat from your Depot?"

"Yes, yes of course."

"We have an understanding then Miss Tyler. Please tell me, how did you know Mr Roberts left the boathouse light on at 11pm?" Her eyes shifted to the wood creaking from the clock housing.

"Come with me Mr Kessler."

Both standing I followed her lead upstairs to the east balcony. Opening the twin doors and stepping out she held the handrail and then pointed.

"Look to where you see the parting of the woodland, the green field that goes to the edge of the lake Mr Kessler. There, follow your eye around the edge." She pointed again and sure enough, there it was, the boathouse.

"Yes, I can see the dwellings. Tell me, what time does darkness ensue at the end of Summer around these parts?"

"Around 9pm Mr Kessler." Gesturing back towards the stairs, we settled again in the living quarters. Reclining on the green couch I dug deeper.

"May I ask, how is your relationship with Mr Roberts?"

"Please drink your tea it will become cold." Drifting over to a dark wooden cabinet she signalled to the framed picture of a sturdy man in a suit. "This gentleman employed Roberts' family over the last century. Karl Braun, my great uncle. When we cut back his responsibilities, Mr Robert's didn't take it so well. Have you managed to speak to him?"

"Briefly yes. I have what I need from Mr Roberts. He seemed, how can I say, greasy. If that makes any sense."

"Yes, yes it is an unfortunate disposition. The poor man."

"How long has he harboured resentment since your decision Miss Tyler?"

"Maybe a little over three years since we last spoke. We gifted him the land and house and freedom to fish on the lake."

My cup clinked touching the saucer. "That sounds like a fair trade. I must say, what a spectacular view you have. I feel like I've been here before, looking out onto the lake."

"Is that all Mr Kessler?"

"One more thing that's been puzzling me. I thought unusual. The fact that it was late, turning dark and then a sprint from two drunken men. Randomly stealing a boat to do what I ask myself? Maybe rushing to get off the land into the water, or maybe to get onto the other side of the lake? Running scared and yet, no sign of the boat or the men. As though they vanished in thin air. So I ask the question. Do you know of any wild creatures in the woodlands?"

Hesitation there was. Miss Tyler's hands intertwined with the nimbling of her fingers. "There was an incident a few years back. If I recall prospectors were getting chased off the land . . . and there was . . . talk."

Peering into her eyes I sensed the uneasiness. A chewing of cheeks as the cogs turned so I employed the silence.

"Familiar but not dissimilar Miss Tyler. In that particular case I believe it was a business matter and land rights. There were two others to my knowledge in the records of strange animals chasing locals in the west of these woodlands." I signalled with my hand as it was in view - on the ridge to the far left of the windows. "Do you remember the Howsen family tragedy a few years ago? This too was right on your doorstep."

"Yes, very unfortunate. Did the Police ever detain the perpetrator Mr Kessler?" Hearing a slight tone change, a reticent response about the woodland creature made a dry aura present. An advantage I thought. Nonetheless, let's not overstay my welcome.

"No there was nobody indicated that I know of. It is still an open case. The gentleman on the wall behind you Miss Tyler. I'm intrigued, please tell me, what was his craft?"

"Why do you ask?"

"He looks strangely familiar too . . ."

"He was a scientist my grandfather. Samual Alderman. A well known literate."

"Do you know of Langton Lodge, the owner of the establishment?"

"Yes, it is Mr Kristof, he knew my father, such a clever man. They both worked together as cryptographers during the war." Pointing to another distinguished looking self portrait.

"There is my father Stefan."

Standing I placed my hat on my head and turned a cufflink. "Yes . . . you have a dignified history Miss Tyler, let's hope we can resolve these surrounding mysteries and keep your good name."

"Thank you detective. The dots you are connecting seem ever more complicated."

"Where you seek you find, that will be all for today Miss Tyler. I will keep you updated, I can see myself out, good day." At a nod and a stroke of the hat the grandfather clock rang past the fifth hour. Enough time to grab dinner at the Lodge.

THE BOATHOUSE

Navigating the winding road and enduring potholes made my return drive tiresome. Leant forward with both hands firmly gripping the wheel to the jolts, I considered that seizing the timely opportunity to investigate the boathouse light was worthwhile. Robert's, the groundsman could be a red herring after learning about the Tyler families feud. Moreover, Miss Tyler had that look that tells me there's more to that story.

As the storm subsided painting a charcoal sky ahead, I took a detour that prompted thoughts about the abandoned schoolhouse. Reaching the hilltop via the old track, I manoeuvred slowly toward the entrance. Peering through a gap in the wooden boards covering the windows made me doubt if it was ever a school. Numerous machines resembling medical equipment, charred, burnt out. The war never reached these parts though, the injured, just too remote. Walking to the south side I lifted a large green sheet covering the entrance of a wood and iron outhouse.

Old tools were scattered everywhere, and a rusty mine cart was no surprise. As I approached the shelves, a scent of freshly chopped wood filled the air - perhaps a week or two old. However, I couldn't discern a fire location. Drawing the sheet down over the entrance, my watch hands were nearly thirty minutes past the hour. I shivered as a cold raindrop edged down the back of my neck. The rolling clouds approached, urging me to swiftly jump into the motor and hit the gas. It's hard to think we scoured a three-mile radius and still no boat or bodies. It's gotta have been dragged out of the water somewhere. Maybe a search around Roberts' part of the lake might yield a result. I gripped the wheel and pushed heavy on the accelerator.

Approaching the Lodge the visibility was down to around hundred feet or so as I turned the headlights to face the entrance. The blue

Chevy must be Miss Biedermann's as I gathered my thoughts taking my case from the trunk, then made a sprint from the rain. The clapping of my shoes in the hallway as I hung my coat on the rack didn't go unnoticed. A familiar tone rang from the seat near the windows.

"Hello Mr Kessler!"

His shadow stood from the end of the desk while the clock chimed and chimed five times for the sixth hour. Pausing to place my hat on the hook and lowering the case. "Ah good evening Mr Kristof. Have I missed anything?" Warm table lights were set for dining with the fire still flamed, Kristof's shadow became visible into the light, peering over his spectacles.

"Possibly a strong drink? May I say Mr Kessler, your timekeeping is impeccable. Please, allow me to show you to your room."

Signalling with his hand, while shouldering my case, I followed him up the stairs, creaking the wooden boards down the corridor to the end - room eight.

"Here's your key. We dine in ten minutes if you are to join us."

Dropping my bag on the bed to the lingering clouds through the bay, I nudged up to the left of the window where the outhouse came into view

- the lights were off. The room was comfortable as expected with bearskins draped over the headboard. Great over the winters etching I thought, luckily I won't be staying to get acquainted. Keeping a sense of urgency, I stripped to the waist for a well needed shave, pulled a fresh shirt from the case and tightened my holster sling and pocketed the Colt inside. Neatening my jacket while exiting the room the hallway echoed with a whirring noise. Turning the key in the lock, in the corner of my eye, the door casing of room twelve emitted a bright light. Curiosity got the better of me as I tip toed towards then held the frame with both hands and placed my ear slowly on one of the panels. An audible jittering, whirring sound, an eerie clunky noise from inside the room, what is that? The hall lights spooked me on the flicker so I stepped away a few paces, touching the wall with my back, sliding down the corridor to clasp the wooden balustrade of the staircase. Taking the first step, my fingertips came into contact with a sticky substance underneath the hand rail. Lifting my hand and peering over the edge I could see what resembled a black tar substance. I picked it from the rail and watched it smooth to a glossy sheen, rolling backwards then forwards in my fingers. Holding it to my nose, an unexpected perfumed fragrance? Folding the tar into a napkin, I placed it into my pocket as my shoes tapped the last few steps of the staircase.

"Mr Kessler" . . . raising his arm towards the decorated candle lit dining table.

"Please be seated. Is the room okay for you?"

"Yes Mr Kristof, it is fine."

"Good good, you must be the fastest shaver in the West!" We laughed together, almost connecting us in rapport. Maybe a helper to opening his clammed history.

"I learned to speed shave during the war. An English guy showed me when we were stationed in Florence. They used to have prizes, mainly a tin of fish for the fastest."

"Were you headed north towards the German Gothic Line Mr Kessler?"

"Yes that is correct." He doesn't know Miss Tyler gave me his cryptographic past, I still need to find a way to draw him out. Pulling my chair towards the dining table and unbuttoning my jacket, I was thinking the setting certainly beats that moat house in Pittsburg on the last case. "I met some great men in the war, what about yourself Mr Kristof? Were you involved?"

Moving slowly while standing to the fire. The orange hue lighting up the front of his face as he stared a void. His head then bowed and with a deep lamenting tone. "Yes . . . yes, there were too many to mention." He slowly gathered a smile, neatening his tie. "Importantly though is our present time. Miss Biedermann should be on her way . . . ahh!"

Our attention towards the staircase as the sound of heels struck the wooden floor. She fitted elegantly in a belted black dress, a pleasant surprise, even Kristof appeared happy as she swooned the staircase onto the last step.

"Good evening Miss Biedermann, how are you?"

"I'm fine thank you Mr.Kristof. I see we have a guest for dinner."

"Hello Miss Biedermann. I must say, you do brush up well."

"Why thank you Mr Kessler. Keep the compliments at regular intervals and we are going to get along just fine."

He drew the chair at the dining table for Miss Biedermann across centre to where I was seated. Kristof became the fawning compère tapping the glass raising his tone.

"We have fresh chicken and vegetables from the near village. Also today the humble potato has featured Mr Kessler. I assumed you weren't a food fuss." Enjoying his trenchant wit in Biedermann's presence.

"I am a simple man Mr Kristof, correct. After dining duck only last week, I'm sure your efforts will be of equal taste." Placing his hands together he sharply quipped.

"Very well I will await your critique. There is water and wine tabled, please enjoy. I won't be a moment."

Kristof made his way to the kitchen and brought dishes, removing the silverware covers one by one to smells that were welcoming.

"Mr Kristof is an excellent cook Mr Kessler. What are you drinking?" Holding a wine in the air I pointed to the darker bottle.

"Red will be fine Miss Biedermann, as long as it isn't corked." He laid his steely eyes my way finishing the serving, after plating the meals he sat to to the left. "We will say thanks."

Toasting our glasses to the quiet start of the dinner, enjoying the warm tones of the fires crackle, I reached for the pepper.

"Do tell Mr Kessler, how is the investigation progressing?" I smiled, picking back my knife.

"Well, there are certain things puzzling me."

"Why do please have another drink Mr Kessler." Kristof interrupted. I nodded, touching my lips to the glass. The leathered skin around his eyes kept me thinking how to uncover the early years after Miss Tyler's insight. Maybe he will loosen up, the evening is early. Miss Biedermann's perfume waving through my senses again, reminds me of something. She continued to question my thoughts.

"So what is puzzling you? I assume joining the dots are ever more complicated?" How peculiar I thought, Miss Tyler rendered the very same sentence over an hour ago.

"There are steps within any criminal investigation. In the cases around these parts, there appears no footprints to make the steps."

"You must have a profile of the individual you are looking for detective?" Resting the cutlery and dabbing my mouth, I clasped my wine.

"Being candid Miss Biedermann. I believe from what I know, there are many people involved. These events appear isolated but the more embroiled I become in my findings, a deeper suspicion keeps fuelling my thoughts. We must turn every page to unfold the story. May I ask . . . what were your movements the day before yesterday, say around six o'clock onwards? Monday the 6th September that is."

"I was 300 miles downstate Mr Kessler. My employer can vouch for me. However, the mine incident happened on Sunday. I assume you are aware?"

"Yes indeed Miss Biedermann."

My question remained open to our host as he unmurmuringly acquiesced. We continued eating and drinking as the air slowly tightened to the chink of silverware, the splinter of firewood and thrashing of rain against the glassed muntins.

"Please, Mr Kristof . . . for the record."

"I was here tending the Lodge." He sharply snapped.

"Too how many guests? I see there are many rooms."

"I had three guests out of twelve Mr Kessler If I recall." He dabbed his mouth slowly. I lifted my brow, glancing at the corner of my eye, he continued.

"Including you and Miss Biedermann, that would be five to date. You could say my sales targets are somewhat down, however it is mid-week. So now, Mr Kessler. May we know the significance of your questions?"

I took the napkin from my lap, laid the cutlery and clutched the wine. “We have two missing people. They vanished on Monday evening, potentially near, or around the lake. The accumulating evidence increasingly suggests murder. One of the individuals is a miner who worked at the collapsed copper mine, we have his name. However, the other man . . . well, there are no records except a note we found in the boathouse on the lake.”

Maybe a facial reaction while narrowing my words to the finish . . . but nothing. The flickering light on both staid faces.

“How can you establish his appearance? The gentleman who penned the note?” Kristof deduced.

“We have a statement who had witnessed both the men running. I have a very adroit field detective, Agent Ryder. He’s looking into his stay in the town.”

“And the words on the note Mr Kessler - what might they say?”

“It seems as though the person was asking for help. The note was not present before the break-in at the boatyard.”

“Well I guess we will have to wait to hear a result.” Twitching his cutlery and adding another guileful redirection. “How is the meal Mr Kessler?”

“Very tasting Mr Kristof.”

“You mean tasteful, surely?” I shouldn’t have doubled up but you know sometimes.

“Gentlemen. I think the word means ‘I’ve yet to finish.’ Would you agree Mr Kessler?” I glanced at Kristof, and while he was breaking a grin couldn’t resist.

“Your timing on the sprouts was a cheer, now please be so kind as to pass the salt.” Miss Biedermann smirked, his countenance getting evermore tightly sprung.

“The two gentlemen you mentioned. What claims can you support that point in the way of murder Mr Kessler?” Inquiring over the top of his glass frames after sampling more wine. I daubed my napkin and contemplated his thought.

“Without jeopardising the enquiry Mr Kristof. You must understand as our previous discussion, everyone becomes a suspect. Frankly, I’m banking on the bodies or the boat appearing by tomorrow morning. A team have already combed the area and found nothing, hence my brief stay at the Lodge. I require a few more parts to the jigsaw. Now, if I may retire the table - the food was great thanks." Pushing back the chair to stand.

"Of course . . . well, my pleasure. Miss Biedermann, I hope you enjoyed."

"Yes, as always Mr Kristof."

Dabbing her lips with a napkin, Kristof eased the chair as she strode to the fire and perched on the edge of the seat. We caught the warmth and beheld the flames dance. A strong sense I had, possibly the need to validate the mine company where she works. Ideally making the long distance call from town in the morning. I reclined to the leather chair opposite while the storm painted the evening light. The frequent chime from the mantled clock resonated. It had become the sounding of the seventh hour.

ENDLESS BEGINNINGS

Kristof continued to age the fire with the brass hamlet while his leather shoe tapped the marble mantle. A cagey intellect with a self-assured hubris, demanding on the pull or push for answers. After hatching that last glass of red I became aware of how many drinks I consumed over the afternoon.

"May I ask for a strong coffee Mr Kristof."

Placing the poker back and brushing his hands. "Yes of course."

He entered the kitchen and politely raising my cheeks, I glanced across to Miss Biedermann.

"The company your associated with, the name? Also if you may, an education in the minerals of interest around these parts."

"Kencott is the company name you seek. We prospect for new mines and over the last decade we have focused on copper acquisitions. One of the key material resources for our governments post war plans. Look at the price of copper ingots Mr Kessler . . . we are living in the modern gold rush."

"So the copper is sought by industrialists?"

"For sure yes. Just like we were the first in the world to draw crude oil out of the ground." Raising her brow. "Nobody knew what to do with it! Eventually being refined into kerosine for lamps, then gasoline to power the engine. Copper will yield the same dominance in the future, the conductive properties are perfect for anything electrical."

Mr Kristof positioned a tray beside me on a smaller table and took a seat next to us. Using the palm of his hand, he gestured toward the coffee cup. I leaned over to add sugar on the stir.

"Very interesting Miss Biedermann. Are you talking about the surge in household items advertised on the highway billboards I keep seeing?"

"Yes the conduit for electrical goods. We supply the copper resource to the merchants with help of the machinery. In the time we live, with the new transport network as I'm sure you understand Mr Kessler, we can deliver to market like never before."

Nodding my head I swallowed a sharp burst of coffee.

"Advancement has been quick since the end of the war for sure Miss Biedermann. As families become more conducive to messaging, let's say for those household items. Do you see the consumption as good in the long term?"

Tasting the wine and folding her black dress near her thigh. Holding up her glass with a jovial laugh.

"It is a philosophical question. I'd say there are far more benefits to having more creature comforts. The war this side of the world helped us grow, to gear up by making equipment for Europe. What I mean is the kickstarting of the military economy, the factories, eventually trickling down to the making of these homestead goods. You are living the rebirth of America Mr Kessler." Her radiant grin catching both myself and Kristof she folded her legs, neatening her hair. "Social orders change as the years flyby. To truly know of any long term changes, you would have to take a journey into the future. Maybe even live for a century or more."

Wearing a stern expression, she directed her gaze towards the flames, casting an orange hue onto the panelled walls. I remained composed as my thoughts lingered. The mention of a future tense, Kristof eluded to this also. They are throwing my compass, they know I'm trying to configure the past to resolve the possible murders. Resuming my coffee, I placed it back on the table, dropped another sugar lump and stirred in the silence while the fire crackle split the air.

"You certainly have good business acumen, and a great drive Miss Biedermann. I wonder if it is good timing that plays a part in the outcomes. In our year, 1956, prosperity is great and I can see the world becoming enriched no doubt. Maybe years from now, a copper machine will serve us drinks!"

We rallied in laughter and small talked the possibilities for a short time. Mr Kristof was cheerfully pouring wine and baiting my thirst. I placed my coffee cup down and heard another guzzle around the glass as my eyes started to wander. I noticed what looked like a tattoo on the right inner ankle of Miss Biedermann's leg. Strange, I thought for a woman of her calibre. Barely visible under her tights, black markings, there, and then gone as she stood from the chair.

"Have you talked to anyone local Mr Kessler?" Her eyes focused on me while striding closer to the chess board.

"Yes, a number of local folk. Yesterday I visited Miss Tyler next to the lake." Perturbed with my meeting Kristof's composure changed, taking his hand from his jacket pocket. Miss Biedermann cradled a chess piece studying the board. I could see it was mid-game. She then placed it into position.

"Shah Mat." She uttered in a soft voice.

"What does that mean per say?" I asked. A chime rang from the tabled clock while her heels clapped the wooden floor with a confident stride towards the window. Her silhouette thrown onto the walled books.

"Shah Mat. It is Persian. It means the King Is Dead."

"I guess you won the game."

"Yes Mr Kessler. The game is all about winning, and please do excuse me for a while." Opening a large door to the right of the window her disappearance was disappointing, if not rushed. The sunlight was meeting the turning way as Mr Kristof reached to the wall lights. The flickering from the wired mains was ever present, making me jittery so I treaded the boards. I gleaned admirably the collection of antiquities. From childhood I vaguely remember working the markets for my stepfathers sister Rosey until entering the army, learning a good breadth of old items. She was an obsessed nut collector, a great blanche for my experience speeding it up. Stretching my arm through two vases I grasped a figurine slightly larger than my hand. An unusual object made of a material hard to describe. I took the opportunity.

"I must say, I recognise many of the items but this one has me stumbled?"

"Yes. I can see that. It is early European Mr Kessler."

Resembling a figure of two bodies intertwined like snakes, but with one head that was finished in what felt, well, flexible . . . skin like. The inscription was barely readable.

"It represents endless beginnings. 'Endlose Anfänge' denotes the inscription you behold, it is from older Germanic writings. At a time when you thought it wasn't plausible for civilised society to understand the human mind . . . it appears some races were ahead of the game."

"Ahead of what game Mr Kristof?"

Reclining opposite in the chair we choked a grin. "Understanding how the mind works, intriguingly though is where it exists. This will always be the tenure for mans exploration. Science, we often think of as a new venture, maybe, was understood from the days of old." I paused, sensing me he could, weighing up his statement. "Your mind Mr Kessler . . . maybe it lives outside your physical presence?"

Lightening and rain followed his voice then the creak of a door and the fasten of a lock slowly turned from upstairs. The pattern of footsteps shunted to a stop at the top of the hallway, then a tardily descent down the staircase. A bespectacled man, unkempt, white braces and an open shirt came into view, a stocky build with a large hat. We made eye contact as Mr Kristof walked closer making hand gestures.

"Good evening Mr Reiner. May I introduce our new guest - Mr Kessler."

I returned the figurine in between the vases and stepped forward, reaching out my hand. He gripped it tight and in a broken English accent made pleasantry.

"Good evening Mr Kessler."

He said he was running into town for supplies and asked what was my purpose at the Lodge - getting to my function point quickly got me thinking he was an engineer.

"A brief stay Mr Reiner. There have been a number of incidents in the area we are investigating."

"Who is we, Mr Kessler?"

His voice was monotoned, what sounded like a European accent for sure. "The Federal Bureau of Investigation." I responded. Immediately the air tightened while his arms slid into his overcoat. Opening the door to a waive of rain, he spoke again in broken English.

"I need to catch the stores before nine o'clock." Nodding to me, then to Mr Kristof on his exit.

"Very well Mr Reiner."

Kristof resumed to the seating area, tapping the flickering wall lights. I hung around the coat rack feeling in my pockets for nothing to catch a glimpse of the black Buick headlights through the entrance glass. The timely tolling of the clock made thirty minutes past seven. I stepped down again into the main room.

“Mr Kristof, may I ask which room is Mr Reiner staying?”

“I didn’t think you hit it off that well you two. Number twelve it is.”

“If I may, as you mentioned on my arrival, the drain on your electric. Mr Reiner’s work, what is it?”

Pacing, fixing his spectacles while cradling his chin. I could sense contemplation in his choice of words. “Experimentation you could call it, or innovation for use of a better term. I think invention would be accurate, and yes, he’s very elusive about his works. I accommodate the flickering and such . . . simply because he pays me more than the other guests.”

I made my way to the windows at the rear knowing I needed to prod more. Glancing to the dark hills while the sun was slowly losing its presence.

“Have you seen Mr Reiner's operation?” He appeared next to me, standing to gaze the rainclouds changing shapes.

“I have an agreement. We both agreed some time ago, that, the key holder to the room can only be himself. An unusual proposition I know but on the merit of payment I obliged.”

"What about the other two guests Mr Kristof. Who are they and their arrangement?"

Relaxing onto the window seat with his brows slightly pulled. "Mr Wiseman. James Wiseman and Miss Taberna. Her first name being Maria. It is a normal arrangement and both have been guests around two months now."

I folded my arms asking the period of Mr Reiner's stay at the Lodge. A reluctant shuffle towards the fire followed by a stuttering reply.

"A little over twelve months. I think from memory."

I know we gave sanctuary to a lot of scientists after the war but Michigan? Something's milling here. Reiner's isolation was a perfect suspect. A hard egg on a long simmer.

"If he needs a good amount of electrical charge could I presume he needs copper? Possibly why his lodging is near a mine?"

Moving to the other side of the desk.

"It may seem like a good deduction detective. However, Mr Reiner creates his own fire and I'm sure he's capable of managing it himself.

"You know full well his comings and goings." Shooting from the hip.

"I have a business agreement and you are the detective Mr Kessler. Why, surely you would prefer the horses mouth rather than the mouses tongue?" A small grin he wore. "I do admire invention, just so you know, it is unique. Rather than work on an established theory, there are no qualifications needed to invent. Intellectual excitement it must be, treading into unqualified areas . . . he earns my respect." Grinning, his response with a smitten overtone. "I can't envisage that cunning wit of yours working with Mr Reiner can you?"

Placing the glass to my lips and meeting his eyes.

"I'm guessing he won't imbrue humour like yourself Mr Kristof. He looks old enough to have been in the war at a glance. Have you come to know him personally?"

"I've come to know him over his stay but that is an extraneous question."

Kristof is just too cagey, gonna have to catch Reiner at some point. While watching the sun descend I ruminated on my next question.

"Do you know Miss Tyler next to the lake?" Sensing the disquieted pause.

"Of course. We have history."

"I must say Mr Kristof, you have an uncanny resemblance to Miss Tyler's grandfather. A misperception on my part maybe."

Unnerved that I made contact. His eyes leering into the wine glass.

"I appreciate your candour about the misconception Mr Kessler."

"I heard you worked with her father Stefan Alderman during the war years. I myself experienced radio comms in the army, intelligence and signal communications. I presume your efforts helped with shortening the war?"

"Didn't everybody's efforts help with shortening the war?" Swirling his glass while the fire flashed his spectacles. "My association started round 1941, there was a programme . . . they named it Eluma. It was there I met Miss Tyler's father. The government were searching for problem solvers in different fields - men and women in engineering, mathematicians, code breakers and the like. People who thought differently and took risks." Slowing his speech while meeting eye to eye. "Not unlike yourself Mr Kristof. You see, I was already working for the military in the navigation rooms so I applied. We had thousands of women helping, the untold success story behind the war results. Miss Biedermann reminds me of some of the sharp intellect we had around us."

As the darkness dropped the landscape behind us to the persistent rain, I assumed he was trying to bring me back to the present tense. I needed to draw him out more.

"Miss Tyler mentioned you and her father solved another mystery while working together."

Scrutinising the flames he slowly turned his head with a smirk. "Why Mr Kessler . . . I doubt if Miss Taylor would be so candid. Seeing as you've stumbled on your words and also the memory of your meeting, what if I were to say yes! We discovered something not known to man."

"Then I would be inclined to ask. What was it you and Mr Alderman had found?" I waited patiently while the fire crackled and he stood. Lighting a candelabra next to the mantled clock, he neatened his jacket and returned adjacent with a softer tone.

"A math Mr Kessler. A very old enigmatic equation that was part written."

"Did it help with the war efforts?"

"Well . . . it wasn't applicable to our government posts. Stefan introduced me to the formulas as I had a broad knowledge of resolving equation problems. I couldn't have done it alone, neither of us could - it did take both our collective efforts."

Nipping the wine silently gazing into the flames. A short time passed.

"Please tell me more about the equation. What was it's purpose Mr Kristof?"

"Have you ever heard of Hookes Law Mr Kessler?"

"Not until now."

"Very well. A physician from England, in the late seventeenth century published his findings on the spring, the springs tension, elasticity and the corresponding displacement effects. A foundation for many disciplines, engineering, mechanics, acoustics, science." Pointing over to my wrist. "The very watch you are wearing has a balance wheel, a coiled spring, thanks to Hooke. The Great Wars have used them in guns to great pity. He had many contributions published . . . all except one. It was while he was performing architectural surveys after the fire of London in 1666. It was there he found something in the rubble, buried, a sealed metal box."

"I'm gonna put my stake in pure luck for the finding." My flippant response made his expression tighten.

"I'd prefer pre-determined fate. Even destiny." He replied.

"Tell me, what's in the box?"

"Notes, diagrams, formulas with many equations . . . everything you could find but with only the right knowledge you could understand. To say lucky would be an understatement." He brushed his jacket lapel. I sensed he wanted to move on. His passion for equations was like sap out of a rubber tree so I kept the train on track.

"The contents of the box Mr Kristof. Please, do continue."

"Stefan's father, Samuel Alderman, he had earlier relatives who worked with Hooke. They passed on formulas that proved invaluable for projects he was undertaking. And so, we completed the passed remnants of unfinished work from both these men."

"How long did you and Mr Alderman work at this?"

"I'd say around three years it had taken us."

"You mentioned Hookes Law, it's disciplines . . . I assume the equation you found fits within them?"

"I'm glad you are listening Mr Kessler, very good. Yes, the end result was an acoustic wave equation. During the war we were searching for oscillations in sound within the radio signals, magnetic waves, just like radar identifies an object. Except we were to find hunting oscillations, like the wheel of a train, when it is out of line, the sounds that didn't fit. To illustrate visually, think of the spark plug within your auto Mr Kessler, the sparking in that space between the coils. In other words, the range within the circuit was vibrating like a tuning fork at its natural, resonant frequency. Of course, in Hertz's circuit the vibrations were not of sound, they were vibrations that are electrically charged. The oscillations in the sound wave, the odd ones, they became the new region in the displacement field we found."

I was intrigued by what importance he laid claim to the findings. "So what relevance does the equation have?"

"My dear friend. It is for all centuries in terms of relevance, for all people. We discovered another mathematical key, more importantly another domain, another realm of existence."

He was writing more confusion onto my face while trying to envisage the invisible from his words.

"I'm sorry Mr Kristof. Please . . . a simpler explanation if you may."

"Very well. The math is a key for unlocking another dimension. Imagine if you have a wave travelling along a rope, the wave has energy and can encode information - backwards and forwards. We tapped into a field along this wave and found the phenomenon."

I knew it was a big achievement but I'm out of my depth. "So what is it? What I mean, is . . . well, what is the phenomenon called Mr Kristof?"

"It is rather difficult to explain, the end application. Maybe tomorrow evening I could relay the experiment, how it works. At this moment, maybe we have had too many drinks to corroborate a successful outcome? Your question though as to what we named our findings, an entry point which we named The Griffin Terminal."

"A Griffin is a mythical creature Mr Kristof."

"Yes. Guarding treasures, that is, priceless possessions."

Deep science it's not my forte but I could see elation on his face and that was enough. Maybe his work is his heart as they say, why is he a Lodge keeper though? He walked past the dining table searching my eyes.

"What would you like to drink Mr Kessler?"

“Another brandy? Where did Miss Biedermann go by the way?”

The clock chimed another bow as I surreptitiously watched him pouring the drinks while gazing the ornate ceiling. I was comfortable albeit the rain and tourney sky revealing the ghostly ring of the moon in the distance.

“She is probably tied up with work. Do I sense a longing for better company.” Smiling while handing me the brandy.

“She fits a dress better than you ever could.”

A brief chortle broke his game then he stepped closer to a wooden box on the mantle, pausing his stance altered. I kept my Colt at the ready. All that talk about springs and coils made me uneasy on his hand movements. Cranking the fire again and reposing in the leather chair he began asking philosophical questions about fate and predetermination. I was intrigued and relayed cases I worked on over the years, to hear a new perspective on the missing pieces of the crimes. Uncannily, Kristof filled in some of the gaps. After a few more chimes of the ebony clock, our deep discussion was at the end of the bottle.

"I'd much rather believe I had free will Mr Kristof. Deciding how I moved forward in life and arriving at my destiny. It has a better ring to it."

He remarked again in his determined tone "One and the same they are, they are both predetermined states. Free will is another illusion of the mind." The fire eclipsing the round spectacles as his eyebrows upraised. "If you were to believe that our conversation is true, then how would you escape your own fate Mr Kessler? Would you choose a different path knowing that you were being led to the same end?"

The rain stopped gabbling on the windows for a minute. Waiting on my breathe, I chewed the fat again. Not the first time since I arrived in this strange abode.

"There doesn't seem to be an answer in my favour Mr Kristof. Unless of course . . . my destiny was a happy end."

"I'm glad we finally agree on something Mr Kessler. Destiny is your void waiting to be filled. Why don't we have a toast to life's journey."

We both reached into the middle still seated and clinked glasses. It was his toast not mine, which I was coaxed into. My thoughts could be tenebrous after the brandy, a little latency waiting for objections that didn't transpire. A moment colluding with my spirit helped with focus, knowing the need for a sharp day tomorrow so I stood from the chair.

"There are several matters I need to take care of Mr Kristof. I'm away early. Who is the early riser in the Lodge?"

"That will be myself Mr Kessler. There will be fresh coffee on the table before your exit."

"I appreciate the service Mr Kristof."

THURSDAY THE NINTH

Waking to the sound of a woodpeckers tenacious knock I automatically clocked the gun from under the pillow. Sharply checking the bathroom and removing the chair from underneath the door knob, the morning routine was done. The clear skies were calming, my head still heavy from the brandy as I buttoned my shirt and tied my shoes. It was approaching nine o'clock. I was late and needed to make the day count. Quietly making my way down the stairs to the hallway, shrugging my coat over each shoulder, I neatened my hat just above my ears.

Kristof wearing a grin sat behind his desk in the mirrors reflection.

"Good morning Mr Kessler. The early bird always catches the worm."

"Not this time. It was a woodpecker who caught me first."

"Are you skipping coffee and breakfast?"

"Today yes. Could you arrange with the other two guests for a chat this evening Mr Kristof? Say in-between five and seven, one at a time. Let each of them know it's a serious matter, now you have the back story. Also last, can you ask for Mr Reiners presence?"

"Yes of course, will you be having dinner before Mr Kessler?"

"I'm not sure where the day will lead so park that."

"Very well Mr Kessler."

I closed out the entrance. The air smelt clean and crisp, the white light and the sound of the trees flexing made the season known. Clicking the trunk handle led me to a wondering stare at the outhouse. A late night gambit I thought to see what's inside. The engine broke the woodland silence as I headed west along the unforgiving road to the town of Hamilton. Let's hope the storm has passed and maybe this time a better reception from the town's folk. After a short ride with not a soul in sight there sat a diner on the outskirts called Red Mill. Parking the brake with a parched mouth I pushed the coffeehouse door and stepped inside. The brunt shudder on the close harboured a few cold stares from the locals while the waitress smiled and pointed to a window table. I nodded, placing my hat on the bench seat.

"So what'll be your order stranger." Flipping her pad while chewing gum I pointed down the menu.

"Yeah the ham omelette, you get coffee with that?"

"You sure do." Writing on the ticket she turned and placed it over the counter, poured the coffee and pointed to the sugar bowl. My head was still heavy so I dropped three lumps in. I sifted through my notebook reading what Mr Roberts was saying about 'this time he called it in'. I wonder how many times he didn't and for what reason? I made light of the omelette and tanked another coffee while occasionally meeting an eyeball from some well oiled regulars. The napkins had a picture of a red mill on the front, I pocketed some and left a tip. The sprung door whined and shunted loosely behind me as I stopped to tie back my shoe lace. Standing to view the clouds reflection running across the glass, through the void, the waitress and other locals were staring back. Opening my door and stretching the leather seat, the door latch clicked into the silence. Placing my hat on the passenger seat I spun the gun barrel to the jolt of the lock and placed it back into the holster. I've arranged to meet Agent Jack Ryder at the mine first thing and I'm brandy late, so the foots to the floor for a few more miles to the outskirts of Hamilton.

Drawing closer to the copper mine, over the hilltops after fighting the muddy terrain there was Agent Ryder, busy addressing a miner. I parked up and trimmed the hat, strolling past the noisy cranes lifting support beams into place, shoring up the collapsed mine entrances. Looked like chaos. Miners were queuing, maybe for wages, maybe for work.

"Morning Dan."

"Good to see you Jack." We shook hands.

"You get the name of the man who disappeared at the Turnpike Depot with the miner?"

"Well, the barman said he was a wood tick from outa town." I aired my confusion . . . "It means a low life round these parts." He said.

Eyebrows raised I paused for a moment.

"A life's a life. He has to have have family. Do you think they just met on the same night as a coincidence?"

"Some of the witnesses said they shifted quite a few drinks. They made their way to the railroad depot near the lake. My take is they were padding down in a carriage for the night. The miner Robert Evans was recently divorced and the other guy they called a wood tick. Well, to date just a forename; Liam."

"Good work Jack. Who oversaw the lake combing for the two men?"

"Agent Clarkson."

"The boat, has it still not turned up?" Clarkson is a stickler for detail so I anticipated a good result from his team and a whirlybird.

"Negative Dan. Been back in touch this morning to the site analysis team. There's something strange about the pieces of clothing found approaching the boathouse and the markings on the door . . . are you ready for this?" He placed a pen in the side of his mouth.

"Try me."

Rolling round his tongue while trimming the hat brow. "They say the markings are that of a bear. The ground prints. The clothing and the door casing of the boathouse."

"How many claws?" I asked.

"Why ask if you've spoken to the lab already Dan?"

Agent Ryder's countenance changed as I nodded my head to the right and we strode amidst the grunting cranes, stopping next to our automobiles.

"I haven't spoke to the site team. I do know bears have five claws."

"Yeah well this one has eight!" he replied.

We both gazed over the ridge into the dense woodland, silently pondering over the findings. The trees stared and swayed our way in their season of change.

"There are many anomalies in life, even possibly in the animal kingdom. Our would be assailant might not be human after all."

Leaning over the roof Agent Ryder was quietly vexed, I guess there was something else. I opened my eyes wider to elicit his concern.

"A chat I had did challenge my thoughts. The folk I interviewed on the outskirts of town near the depot. They said, you know, all that talk about folklore . . . but they were accurate with the times without knowing what had happened." He turned the pages of the notebook to read aloud his description. "This is exactly like for like Dan." 'The panicked screams of men we could hear as they were running. We bolted the windows and doors and hid in the attic. Another deep and loud voice was shouting them down, it was that of another man.' "I asked what the shouts were . . . they replied," 'he kept saying help me.'

Our eyes met bewildered. Our focus frozen on the woodlands, scanning from left to right. Tapping the roof metal I had to call it in.

"We need some sharp shooters up here asap. If there's a beast on the loose we need to check with the Sheriff in town. Escaped animals, huntsmen sightings, you know, reports of that nature." Peering into the void of the forest. "The note in the boathouse - did it say 'help'?"

"Yes. It was penned handwriting. What are you thinking Kessler?"

"Jump in. Show me where the long distance wire is . . . I gotta check something."

After a short drive we rode into Hamilton. It was bustling with people and automobiles zooming up and down the broadway. The mine must have brought many traders as stores lined the walkways.

“It’s all Babuchi round here.” Agent Ryder remarked.

“You’ll have to translate that.”

“It means relaxed upstate here. That’s what the local folk told me.”

We parked outside the gift shop, to the right he pointed to the postal office.

“There’s a wire in there, long distance. I’m gonna grab a bite and a coffee you want a shot?”

"Yeah Jack pour the sugar in, I guess it's gonna be a long day. Gonna check on one of the guests from the Lodge and update my progress."

Closing the door on the Post Office I neatened my jacket and asked for the long distance wire. Over in the corner I pulled a chair to the booth, opened my notepad and rang the operator.

“Hi, can you patch me through to a quarry merchant called Kencott? Around Detroit possibly?”

“Okay sir please bear with me.” I listened to the pips for a couple of minutes before a response. “We have a listing but we can’t get a connection from the other line.”

“How would you know if it’s dead the line?”

"The usual dead tone sir. The lines active, but our records show a number change two years ago. That usually means a change of business."

"Okay thanks. Can you patch me through to 950 Pennsylvania Avenue - Washington DC - 20530."

"Department of justice sir?"

"Yes please, thanks." I checked in with FBI headquarters and updated my case, not many gains so far. Passed the quarry details on for further checking and was told military snipers will arrive Friday evening. The heat was on to close the case before a panic from the town's folk. The local Sheriff, Wyatt Dalton hasn't cooperated so I was told to shore him up. After an hours chat on the updates, squaring off and nodding to the clerk - Agent Ryder gave me a coffee and we headed over to the bar where the missing men were last seen.

The landlord was sharp faced and deliberately vague so we took a table and waited patiently for regular daytime drinkers. We gathered small talk for a few hours but not much to glean from eye witnesses'. Jack's hunch of the men sleeping at the Depot railroad carriages was confirmed. On mention of a possible bear sighting, there was an eerie silence and a guarded response. A taboo subject with the locals. The gaunt eyeball from the Landlord told me we were bad for business, so I tipped the bartender and we stood under the canopy on the porch watching the traffic.

"Do you think it's a deep religious place here Jack?"

"No Dan it ain't religiously rooted. You know as well as I, someone or some bunch of people are running this town."

"Yeah the bear's a touchy subject for sure, nobody wants in. Let's see what Sheriff Dalton has to say. Which way Jack?"

He pointed down the Broadway to the corner building backing up onto the river. Moving through the stalls on the walkway we slowly approached the jailhouse. Shouldering some cold stares from the deputies loitering the benches outside I nodded and tipped my hat towards the entrance. The groan of the door didn't stoke the Sheriff's attention as we stepped inside the dated interior. Tasting the dust I choked a snicker and made our presence known.

"Good day. I presume it's Sheriff Dalton?"

Seated, boots hanging over his desk, leather jacket and nose down under his hat with both hands ringed on his stomach, he moved his head slightly.

"That'll be me."

Our shoes scuffed the hollow wooden boards as the door latch sounded and we stood in the silence. Behind him was a picture framed of the schoolhouse besides others of the town. A long pause as I glanced at Ryder knowing Dalton was waiting for us to show our hand.

"Were here to solve the missing people mystery around these parts Sheriff Dalton. We'd be grateful for your help. This is Agent Ryder, Jack Ryder. I'm Detective Dan Kessler."

I know he's a straight shooter. Looks like he's been coasting for some time in a small town. He didn't move, just a finger tap while his head raised slowly.

"You know what happened to the last detective who came round these parts don't ya?" Pushing his hat to eyebrow level, his finger running his moustache. Continuing alongside the creak of a wooden chair. "He went missing didn't he Kessler?"

I stepped forward from Agent Ryder. Jack looked confused, he must not know all the goings on around here from the past. I kept my hands in my pockets.

"Well I guess we should start there. We still haven't found answers for his disappearance . . . was it Tayler? Detective Ewambes?"

"You should know Detective Kessler . . . why he came from the same place as your kind. Poking his nose in to this town's business."

I need to play his bluff. "I did hear he was last seen at the old schoolhouse."

His boots scraped the desk and hit the floor with both hands on the chair arms. Standing adjusting his belted jeans, he lifted his arm and pointed to the end of his opposing desk.

"Grab a seat both of ya."

We parked ourselves on the beach spindled chairs while he flicked open a silver whisky flask. Swigging a shot and screwing back the top with intense eyeballs locked onto us, he sat with his elbow on the desk pointing his finger.

"Now I wanna get this clear to you agent folk for the tenth time. That was never no schoolhouse. I called it out before the war and nobody listened."

"I'm sure the bureau . . ."

"Never mind the bureau this and that detective." Stopping my train he leaned back in his creaky chair, pointing to a picture on the wall. "I used to play round these parts as a boy.

That's me and my best friend Wyler. We had some great times you know, pass the old farmers yards and the lake. That's him with the Stetson wearing the big happy smile." Looking twice back to the picture, Dalton's long stare was intense. "You had any good friends Kessler? I mean close friends."

"I struggle remembering my childhood Sheriff. Maybe it was the war."

"Yeah well, my memories are intact. Wyler was a happy soul. He grew into being a great engineer. The best!" Raising his tone and running his tongue under his moustache. "He just had that brain you know, he understood them things. Guess they don't make machine engineers in the city do they Kessler."

We fixed eyeballs over a dusty silence.

"No . . . that's correct Sheriff Dalton."

He leant forward with intensity. His leather jacket creasing, placing his hands together turning his thumbs.

"Yeah. That's right. You have too engineer out here to survive. Wyler was one of them. He disappeared like your last detective." His lips scrunched at either side, his jacket creased like a tightening rope. He appeared agitated while adjusting his hat.

"I'm sorry to hear about Wyler. What year was his disappearance?"

Tapping his fingers, hands upright while rocking. Working us out he was. "Around three years ago . . . the schoolhouse owners hired him to work on the machines they had." He kept his suspicious stare and rolled his tongue behind his moustache. I knew it wasn't a schoolhouse when I looked through the windows.

"Who owns the deeds to the land, the schoolhouse property?" I asked.

"There ain't no record like that detective."

"When was the last time you investigated the place?" I replied.

"Three years ago we did. We shut that place down good . . . it's been bordered up ever since." His smirk said something as we both observed the schoolhouse picture. I know out here they deal with folk in one swoop. Kill or be killed.

"Tell me Mr Dalton, what happened to your friend Wyler?"

"They killed him."

"The Schoolhouse owners. Is that what you mean?"

"They butchered his soul first . . . stripped him of the man he was. Treated him like a dog." Raising his vocal to a growl. "Them machines he worked on were different. They weren't tractors that's for sure Kessler."

My eyes at Jack, both of us squinting in the spit. I guess Ryder's still wondering about the other detective previously here that Dalton mentioned. Reading through the lines I guess it was a shootout on the hill of the schoolhouse with Dalton and his deputies burying the bodies on the board up. He's not a stones throw away from Kristof when it comes to answering questions, his eyes are much craftier.

"The machines? What was their purpose?"

A squinted sizing up at one another while Dalton's moustache moved with his tongue. Tapping his fingers, once then twice, faster and faster.

"They were putting people inside them . . . that's right . . . people! Now we do that with animals round these parts at the slaughterhouse. Those machines we set on fire! All of um. Was pure evil what they were doing. We asked the Feds for help and they sent one detective down. That's right one!" He banged his fist hard on the desk cursing a scowl showing his teeth. "Wyler would have still been here if your man would had done his job. He was around for three days and disappeared like a twenny dollar bill in a whorehouse. Call yourself what you want Kessler, agents, detectives . . . it's a different spine from the city. I think y'all got less vertebrae than us country folk."

Holding onto his sentiments for a minute or two until he regained composure and took a seat. I noticed a receipt from the mine on the desk, prompting me to press.

"Sorry to hear about your friend Wyler. I can empathise. A question about the collapsed mine Sheriff Dalton. Do you purchase copper from there?" Moving my eyes towards the receipt.

"An investment detective."

"Robert Evans, one of the miners missing, do you know of him?"

"Yeah, I knew his father, died in the war. Evan's been down the whisky house ever since. I seen your folk around the lake. You find his body?"

"No . . . not as yet." I replied and thought I'd throw him an invite.

"I've arranged to go back with another search party. Army snipers are scheduled to arrive in about 36 hours. Maybe the thing in the woods is the answer to the missing persons?"

Now began the silence . . . an empty cave waiting on the raindrop. He stayed sturdy as a wood log, we all did. Felt like an hour before the door swung open loud. His deputy asked 'Is everything okay Sheriff?'

"Rydell - take a hike."

Dalton threw his voice towards the door. And then began another silence. A minute or two passed inside the Dalton void . . . the odd creak from his chair stare . . . the rolling of his tongue and tautening of leather. He knew that we knew, he had some knowledge of a beast in the field. He wasn't for turning though Dalton, his game was too sharp. A bead of sweat from under my hat rolled down the side of my cheek - I had to break the silence.

"Help us catch this thing Dalton. Maybe, just maybe . . . it will be an easy hunt." Throwing caution to the wind. I moved focus to his rifle rack hoping he'd feel the call of duty. He's a dirty player and likes a result. His glare was cold and hard and then a small twitch, a glint of excitement from his right eyeball.

"Huntings a strong word coming from a city boy Kessler." He rocked another chair creak while leaning forward. "Have you any, any idea how to handle a rifle Kessler?"

"I was stationed in the thick and the deep all the war and survived. The hunt will begin a day from now - can you join us?"

He swivelled, turning to the window where the line of light was.

"Those gun racks look dusty Sheriff. Whatever happened in the past is gone. We won't go there. We'd appreciate you and your men up on the ridge southeast of Miss Tyler's home on Saturday."

"They ain't dusty Kessler that's the glass housing. The lady of the lake that Miss Tyler, she ain't no lady just so you know detective. Yeah we'll be there sunrise . . . also . . . it's Sheriff Dalton to you Kessler." Swinging back facing off with his stiff persona. Intense, like he was touching my eyeball.

"Appreciate your help . . . Sheriff Dalton."

We lifted the corner of our lips and almost smiled. Both Jack and I headed towards to the door. I turned and Dalton touched the brow of his hat, we had an agreement for Saturday. Stepping off the Sheriff's porch we were carried by the deputies cynical stares into the noisy streets. Heading back to our drive the air eventually quietened as I knew what was on the tip of Jack's tongue.

"Who's the last detective on the case around here Dan?"

"His name was Detective Tayler Ewambes. He disappeared after three days out here. The Bureau has nothing, no sightings. They conducted interviews, you know, nobody knew nothing." We landed at our ride and sat in the calm having a relieving gasp.

"Wow. Dalton's a tough cookie - my eyes are burnt."

"That's right, them eyes could spot a ground squirrel from three miles. Stay alert, keep sharp around here Agent Ryder. Keep that gun at the ready." He nodded and had a hand on his heart and one on his ankle Colt.

"Do you think they'll show up on Saturday. Dalton and his men."

"Yeah he can't wait to go hunting again. A motley crew Dalton and his deputies. The Lodge I'm staying at Jack, do some digging over the long wire. The owners a guy called Kristof. Michael Kristof. See how many years the Lodge has been operating. Also see if a surname called Reiner appears anywhere. Possibly Hans, his first name, he's European for sure."

We stopped for gas and rang the bell. The service man walked closer, leaning in the window smiling.

"Thirty two cents - how many gallons sir?"

"Ten gallons and here, keep the change."

"Thanks good sir."

He tapped twice on the car roof after filling the tank. We headed back to the quarry to drop Agent Ryder off. We journeyed a bumpy ride for a while until I brokered a plan.

"Tomorrow Jack we check the schoolhouse. Whatever we find is between us understood?" Turning he gave me the nod.

"Dalton can keep the memories. I've peered through the schoolhouse windows and it ain't no education centre. Maybe we will find one of those machines the Sheriff kept barking about, the machine that changed his friend . . . Wyler."

Jack lifted his arm, pointing at the road ahead, we swung left as the trees broke onto the steep quarry track. Edging ever closer to the ridge upon the hill, the white light from the September sun flashed the windscreen. We slowed to almost walking pace as many workers and their wagons started drifting our way from the top of the hill. The mud thickened on the track and we ground to a halt. They looked cold and hungry as we watched in silence waiting for the pass. Tapping my fingers on the top of the wheel my patience thinning.

"Have you spoke to any of the wardens or the mine manager?"

"Yeah the warden was available but couldn't get near the manager this morning for the chaos. It's late afternoon so we've got a chance. Looks like the workers are leaving. The mine manager is Mr Rigg, his cabin is the one stilted with the balcony overlooking the others."

We struggled getting around the corner of the on the ridge, our rides back end was sliding for a few minutes until we hit the steady stone track on the entrance to the quarry. We looked at each other and gave way to a laugh, grounding ourselves into reality briefly. The cabins became visible near the mines entrance where cranes were still hoisting materials from the ground. Parking up we asked a worker for Mr Rigg. He pointed to the top of the tall stair balcony on his cabin. There must have been at least 100 stairs as we both clanked the steel risers and heavy footed, gasped a breath onto the last rung. I removed my hat and wiped my brow and the door opened quickly on the cabin. A small man suited with a sharp tone asked our credentials.

"Has the site warden given you permission to my cabin?"

"He hasn't no sir. I assume it's Mr Rigg? We're Federal Agents, here investigating events around this area, may we?" I opened my hand towards the inside of the cabin.

"Yes, yes come inside. Excuse my rudeness, it has been the worst time in the history of the mine."

The cabin was neat with a dusty film. I watched the crane through the window trying to edge another beam in place while Agent Ryder introduced us and asked if he knew of the miner who was last seen at the turnpike depot.

"Yeah, Robert Evans. I know him. He's a putter."

I turned back towards Mr Rigg and stared a blank as he filled the gap.

"It's a man who helps the loaders and the hurriers, he helps with carts inside the mine. I know every individual worker on the payroll, Robert has a good work ethic, always shows up . . . I wish some of the other men would."

"Well, he's one of the men missing on the lake." Jack informed him.

I stared out of the south view of the windows over to the forest while Mr Rigg turned in his chair hearing the news.

"That's a shame to hear. I mean, are you suggesting foul play Mr Ryder?"

"We can't be sure Mr Rigg. There were two men, possibly drunk in a boat on the lake, late on the night of the disappearance. We have no boat and no bodies."

"Let me make a reference to pay the wages owed to his family members."

He took his pen and scribbled down a note in the payroll book. We heard a large thud followed by a bang and Mr Rigg stood, moving quickly to open the door. A number of men were gathered around a hoist as he leant over the balcony rail and began shouting.

"Be careful with that dragline! There's enough butt cleat near here to cause another collapse." Raising his arm in a circle with a finger pointing upwards he was signalling to wrap it up. Still flustered he closed the door, pulled on the collar of his shirt and sat back behind his desk.

"Excuse the interruption gentlemen, please continue."

I pulled a chair closer to his level and asked if he had the ledger of his accounts over the last 12 months. Hesitant, leaning back he then grabbed a file from the left drawer of his desk and slowly handed it to me. I looked at Agent Ryder and nodded, it was his turn to ask the questions. Searching through the pages I turned to the index of businesses. Mr Rigg kept eyeballing me while being questioned. My finger ran down the list until there it was, Kencott Incorporated. Miss Beiderman's workplace.

"Sorry Jack, let me interrupt. Mr Rigg please, the purchases of copper back in July from Kencott Incorporated. I met with someone recently he went by the name of Mr Sheldon, a representative who mentioned this mine. Do you know of him?" Playing his bluff I could see he was confused.

"I'm sorry Mr Kessler. I've never heard or met a Mr Sheldon. I do know of a Miss Biedermann from Kencott, one of the only women who buys from us."

I guess it's confirmed she was telling a truth. Whether that's the whole truth though, I'm still dubious.

"We get regularly lied to in our trade Mr Rigg . . . I'm sure you can understand."

"Why yes of course." A grinned reply that improved as I closed the ledger and handed it him back. Jack finalised the formalities and jotting the last of his notes. I turned to Mr Rigg.

"Just one more thing. Kencott Incorporated the company, do you have a registered address or maybe a district location?"

"We just take the money Mr Kessler. Dollar is our fuel."

"How long before the mines up and running again?"

"Difficult to say Mr Kessler. Possibly three months, but we can't wait that long the winters coming. The crane lines will freeze and, without the road being used regularly, nobody will be able to access the mine. A month I'd say possibly we could stand." He rolled the pen in his left hand, tapped it on his notebook while raising his brow, gazing toward the windows he concluded. "Let's see how they get on. The locals need the work, and we need the copper."

I turned to Agent Ryder and trimmed the front of my hat. With a nod of my head, we both stood and looked across the desk. "That will be all for today Mr Rigg."

Negotiating the slippy metal stairs outside the cabin was more arduous than the climb. Our fingers frozen white to the hand rail as we stepped into the mud after the bottom rung.

Each of the pooled water ditches could have been easy three feet deep so we made a tip toed dance towards the wardens cabin where Jack was parked. Getting closer to his auto a black film of coal enveloped the body. Laughing at one another while rubbing our finger lines to clear the windows. The time was closing in four o'clock. I requested Jack visit Miss Taylor's place so not be alarmed when we meet there on Saturday. Behind the wheel, he wound the window while I leant both hands on the door. I took a few deep breathes, signing off for the day.

"Tomorrow Agent Ryder, ten o'clock, morning fresh at the bottom of the hill at the schoolhouse. Give you chance to catch the distant wire at the postal office first thing. Stock up, let's be cautious."

"Sure will Agent Kessler. You tapping to the Lodge?"

"Yeah, my gut says something at the Lodge don't stack up Jack. The air smells crisp. The trees are changing colour. We're in the middle of the game. Let's get to the end."

THE ENTANGLEMENT

The ride to the Lodge almost felt too smooth this time. My watch was approaching thirty minutes past the fifth hand and the sun was fading. I kept wondering about the detective who disappeared after three days, he never wired over any findings and the local folk had no recollection of him.

The Lodge was shrouded in smoky rainclouds. I switched off the lights, drove past and parked the car amidst the dense woodland. I snuck amongst the trees, handled my gun and shuffled to the outhouse. Appearing as a weathered wooden structure, it resembled an old car garage or a groundsman's workshop. Approaching within 50 yards, the abrupt squawk of a raven prompted me to swiftly drop to my stomach. Above me, on the treetop, the raven was peering down it's beak knowing the fright ditched me into the wetland. A light appeared from inside the outhouse, I was spooked briefly wondering if it was controlled from the Lodge. I waited patiently for a rustle of the bushes or any signs of life, nothing emerged. Rising with a coat now smeared with mud I cautiously approached, leaning against the wooden boards then slowly advanced towards the entrance door.

"Stop," I muttered to myself upon hearing footsteps, resonating from a stone floor. Drawing nearer, I crouched, scanning my surroundings for cover. The footsteps intensified as I pressed my ear against the wood, my right arm holding the gun upright.

Someone stepped towards the exit from the inside. I froze as the handle jolted and the hinges groaned, jarring the door to a close with the clicking of the lock. I held my breath as shoes scuffed the stone entrance slab. Hanging in the balance I felt relief as the footsteps diminished, heading towards the Lodge. Squatting to the edge, I peered around the corner and to my surprise it looked like Miss Biedermann. It was Miss Biedermann! Placing my back onto the outhouse and gazing skyward I needed a moment to catch my breath. Despite the confusion, I was aware of having lock picks in the trunk, perhaps not the opportune moment. Returning to the car, I settled on the cold leather, taking ten minutes to regain my composure. I retrieved additional ammo from the dashboard and tucked them inside the pocket of my jacket. Wiping the mud from my shirt and trousers the engine groaned as I rolled up to the exterior of the Lodge.

The echo of the entrance bell sharpened Kristof's movement. His shadow on the panelled walls changed direction as he closed into eye contact.

"Hello Mr Kristof, how are you?"

"Yes, fine thank you." My soiled clothes didn't go unnoticed.

"You haven't been trying to rescue hogs running off cliff edges have you Mr Kessler?" His sarcastic smile becoming familiar by the day. I had to think on my feet.

"Pushing the bucket at the copper mine wasn't planned."

"Let me take your jacket to place on the rail near the fire."

"Very well, can I bustle another coffee?" His silent nod made my hand point to the drinks bay, "May I?" Pouring a calming brandy I thought maybe it was the one hundred steps up to Rigg's office, or the precarious road ahead. The liquor shot helped warm my blood and cancel todays aberrations. A flamed shadow on the bookcases resembled wings recalling the griffin, the terminal Kristof says he's found. Maybe the terminal exists in or around this Lodge I got to thinking. He wandered over taking the chair, closing the space while I lingered fireside.

"How did the detective work progress today Mr Kessler?" His question. Was it a genuine path from his compassion? His raised brows and sarcastic tone made me think otherwise.

"Very well. Very well Mr Kristof."

"Did you find the men missing on the lake?"

"Not yet. There's a search party arranged for Saturday at dawn . . . if you care to join us?" He smiled and a chuckle returned his lips to a close.

"My dear Mr Kessler . . . have I to bring the sandwiches at lunchtime?"

"Your kindness knows no bounds. No salmon from the lake until we find the bodies."

His expression shifted as he extended his hand

to an open box of cigars resting on the table before us.

"Indulgence some may say Mr Kessler, however I would call it focus." The sound of the flint from the lighter choked. A ring of smoke drifted between my eyes tasting the sweet leaf again.

"Excellent flavour Mr Kristof. Excellent."

"For a moment I thought you uttered 'your excellency' Mr Kessler."

"Your hearing, maybe once a cliff-top radio receiver could now be perceived as a residential woodland murmur."

"Your metaphoric satire sound like ramblings of a Laureate poet Mr Kessler. Please enjoy."

Both of us in good spirits, he gestured toward the drinks bay, prompting me to request a black coffee. Kristof prepared the coffee while I traversed the room. The sun's rays, filtering through the clouds, gently passed by my shoulder. The shimmering of the books caught my eye, like a school of fish, a metallic vibrancy in the lights presence. I circled his desk and had a clear view of his work station, his number scribbles littered the papers.

"Mr Kristof . . . the digits on the desk. Are they co-ordinates may I ask?"

"Yes that is correct." His silhouette fireside, smoke rising from the chair.

"Are they directions to the Griffin Terminal?"

"A good question detective. Your work never stops does it?" He peered around the leather chair. "They are directions within the Griffin Terminal. Yes, they are to navigate."

I stepped closer to the crackling flame naturally intrigued, flushed the sinuses with the last drop of brandy and casually parked myself. Reaching for the coffee Kristof was baiting me with his calm composure.

"What are you looking for inside the Terminal?" I asked.

"Gates Mr Kessler. Not doors . . . gates."

"How many gates have you come to know?" He exhaled a large smoke ring into the air, breaking apart into the flames above the mantle.

"Very good Mr Kessler. We are making progress. Six gates to the present day. Although the sixth hasn't been found . . . or entered, only it's existence acknowledged. The elusive one's are the seventh and eighth gates. We know they exist somewhere inside the Terminal."

A doting pleasure of his - observing the confusion written on my face. Intrigued with my interest I have to keep feeding him the chum and get to the bottom of my agenda.

"Who is the 'we' Mr Kristof?"

"There are many of us."

The clock chimed another movement to fifteen minutes past the fifth hand. Embracing the coffee cup warmth made me wonder if Kristof, and the other guests staying are the many? The sun was grounding, switching into early evening, darkening the living space. Placing his cigar in the ashtray he fiddled with the wall lights to a flicker, reaching for a glass lamp towards the chess board table.

"Tell me, what is actually inside the gates you have found? What is there purpose, there importance?"

Rotating the brass notch on a kerosene lamp, his face warped through the glass housing he replied.

"Very good Mr Kessler. Your intriguing questions are not without expectation. May I suggest a more suitable time later this evening so you can fully comprehend these findings."

"Very well Mr Kristof. Have you informed the guests about my request?"

"Yes, unfortunately Miss Taberna and Mr Wiseman have appointments to seat. Although they might return later tonight, we'll have to wait and see Mr Kessler. However, I have spoken to Mr Reiner, he will be available. Would you prefer something to eat first?"

I strode across the hearth to the brazen windy howl and creaking timber beams.

"Yes, another large coffee with a few slices of toasted bread if I may."

"Excellent, I will accommodate." His eyes squinting as the flames reflected across both glass lenses. "Could you please place more logs on the burner, it may become another cold night."

Approaching the fire, one by one I fuelled the flames with chopped timber from the storage. The natural light through the windows began to decay as I nudged the brass poker into the red embers.

"Mr Kristof. What's the probability of both Miss Taberna and Mr Smith having business appointments at the same time on the same day?"

As he neared, positioning the food and drink onto the table top, he paused shifting his head towards me.

"Very high if they both work for the same corporation."

"Very well. A moment please Mr Kristof to gather my thoughts."

He nodded, retiring to his desk while I sat and ate. He didn't mention previously the two guests working together, but then again, I never asked and my stay at the Lodge was random. After another clock chime I asked Kristof for Reiner's company in the living quarters. It was difficult to gauge his age, Reiner, I'd say in his fifties, peculiar looking, bespectacled and this time around - smartly dressed. He asked for hot water while lifting the cigar box case and raising his expression at Kristof. We gave way to small talk about the antiquities inside the Lodge keeping him relaxed, smoke in hand while Kristof kept the heat radiant. The coffee made me jittery so I plumbed for another brandy while surrendering to a sweet taste of the cigar leaf.

Reiner moved to the chess board and began setting up the pieces. Offering his hand to the opposing chair for a game. Accepting, I tabled my brandy and we entered into the respectful silence. A slow burner through the opening stages until inevitably we locked at a critical point. The walled pawns shielded us both as the escalation of an attack approached. With our backs to the chairs we gamed a foreboding stare.

Reiner's wrinkled eyes behind the spectacles never blinked.

"I believe it's your move Mr Reiner."

"I assume your a few moves ahead and know my possible options."

"Let's see what happens."

"Knight takes bishop Mr Kessler."

"The knight is a crafty piece. I speculated on your retention." He reclined into his chair with a toothless grin. Reaching for the drink and chewing his lips he uttered a broken English response.

"I was thinking of the end game. To be blind sided on the diagonal could be punitive. Sometimes you forget the bishop is there, waiting for you to make a wrong move."

"Pawn takes Knight."

"Queen takes Knight."

Damn, I didn't see that coming. The Queen was out of sight, now looming over my castled King.

"Maybe your concentration would work better for your own game Mr Kessler. Rather than focusing on mine."

"Maybe you are more cunning than I Mr Reiner. The game has many surprises. "Pawn to Rook three." Threatening his Queen made him crouch forward into focus. Exercising patience as minutes passed I searched for a transmission. "Mr Kristof mentioned your inventiveness. I am curious about what it is you do."

Wearing a serious expression while placing his Queen a few squares back. His head still facing the board his eyes rolled upwards.

"Yes Mr Kessler. Queen to Rook three."

Hmmm I guess another hard egg simmer. Gonna have to play the slow game and lift the hood gently. "May I ask what it is that you invent?" No sooner had the words left my mouth, the poker in Kristof's hand clunked against the hearth as Reiner shifted focus towards the fire. His hands intertwined, sensing I could, the reluctancy of my question.

"Objects. Mr Kessler. I invent objects."

That accent I just can't place, a little wooden round the edges. Okay I don't mind another few rounds I thought, he's a seated enquiry. A tightening of the air as I leant forward to make my gun accessible while studying the board. His shrewd responses are baking my suspicion, or he's just a cold card.

"Knight to Rook four." A move closer to breaking down his defence. Maybe he won't foresee my plan.

"What type of medium do you use to craft the objects Mr Reiner?"

"Metallurgy." His hand lifting the end pawn. "Pawn to Rook three."

Kristof swivelled the leather chair near the fire and perched, folding his legs with glass in hand, his sharp shoe pointing towards me. I had an unnerving sense about his intentions but need to relax, maybe I was overthinking. Looks like Reiner's uncovered my schema. I need to know what materials he's using? "Pawn to Knight three. Is it just the one metal Mr Reiner?" We all rode out the silence. Cautiously perched on the edge of my seat I tippled another small wet of liquor. Reiner continued chewing his lip, attending the structure of his pieces. Kristof's reflection appeared in the corner of my eye, seated at the mirrors edge.

"There are several combined metals . . . an alloy to be precise." Reiner stated head down, focusing on the board. An object made from an alloy had me thinking of ammunition.

"I never took you as a watchmaker Mr Reiner. As Mr Kristof stated; curiosities can lead to assumptions. That makes me ask - what objects become from the metal alloy?"

The clock chimed and chimed again. We were fort five minutes past the sixth hour as evening broke. A few shuffles from Reiners feet and an occasional stroke of his knuckles as the games stillness gathered latency from my previous question. The Lodge creaked as the fire snapped a crackle so I shifted my butt slowly around, unbuttoning my jacket. My surreptitious eye at the mirrors edge on Kristof presiding over us.

"You are correct, I am not a watchmaker Mr Kessler. One of my specialities is the making of guns. Pawn to Bishop five."

I was taken back. My gut told me otherwise though so no surprise. Still embroiled in the game, a new phase we were entering. Slowly reaching out my hand for my move. "Queen to Bishop four . . . I presume you were skilled as a gunsmith during the war Mr Reiner?" Assessing me while mildly stroking his thumb and fingers across his forehead. Another fleeting glance my way, then back to negotiating his game.

"Correct Mr Kessler. It is a family affair. My work seeded over generations, henceforth the inventions. New blood into the craft you could say."

"Would your family be European or American?"

"Bishop to King four." Pleased with the choice move through a revealing grin, his fingers closed around the brandy glass. A swirl under his nose made both eyes sharpen, "Austrian," he remarked and swilled the balance. Kristof proceeded to take the brandy bottle from the drinks bay and stood varnishing Reiner's glass. Nudging the tipple I had another potion poured and after a brief chug caught Reiner's eye.

"If I recall, Austria was part of the German Confederation." My senses were tingling. The tapping of Kristof's shoes on the wooden floor came to a halt. Then the creasing sound of the leather chair assuming his position. Reiner set down his glass on the table and tilted a coin between his knuckles. Keeping my head straight on the game I relied on fleeting glances knowing alloys for guns needed copious amounts of copper. It's all making sense now. He's smithing sticks in room twelve and Kristof knows it.

"You would be correct in your recollection." Reiner confirmed.

"Pawn takes Pawn Mr Reiner." I positioned the piece next to the others previously taken for a peer into the mirror at Kristof. "Would I also be correct that the German army was weaponised through your inventions?" We entered another stillness. Awaiting his gambit, lifting my drink to Kristof's warped reflection at the mirrors edge, I freed the opposite hand to access my gun.

"Well it seems we have an equal exchange value in the game. I shall return the move. A Pawn for a Pawn Mr Kessler."

"An eye for eye we'd call that in the war Mr Reiner." Nobody moved. The stint of wood turning on the burn in the background. I didn't want to take my eyes off Reiner's cunning grin.

"You see, my family I cannot choose. Georg Luger was my father."

"I witnessed many deaths at the hands of a Luger." My response sharp and candid as my hand tightly gripped the glass, feeling heated around the collar. What is a German gun manufacturer doing out here in the Michigan woods? My intuition knows more than my thoughts, maybe he's Kristof's stool pigeon. The clock chimed on the seventh hour, followed by another five as the coin flipped to the end of Reiner's knuckles and landed on the maple floor with a sharp ringing sound. Spinning to a blur, then slowly but surely stopping to a clink.

"Id much rather refer to our families historical work as the Austrian Luger pistol. Addressing your earlier question Mr Kessler. We manufactured guns for the German army in both wars. Unfortunately, I was never really a good shot with the pistol. My skills were always in the manufacturing. However . . . Mr Kristof is an excellent shot."

Reaching the turning point. Peering into the edge of the mirror where it fades and bends. The fire flashed Kristof's seat with the metal glint from a gun barrel pointing my way. Reactively on the draw my right hand moved to grab the Colt from inside my jacket.

"DON'T DO THAT KESSLER!" I froze. Time stopped as I slowly shifted my head towards Kristof chair. Motionless, smirking, pointing a Luger within his left hand.

"STAY STILL." He bawled.

"Please . . . Mr Kessler, let me take a look. I assume it's a Colt 38?" Reiner voiced conceitedly.

"CAREFUL NOW Mr Kessler . . . very slow. Hand him the gun, butt first. Keep your eyes on me. NOT Mr Reiner." I played ball damn. Two seconds too late on the draw, it was suspected but unexpected. I've still got my ankle glizzy, so will have to wait for the air to crack.

"Now the Model 13 from the ankle strap Mr Kessler. VERY SLOW. Butt first to Mr Reiner. EYES ON ME." He waved the barrel sideways for the order. No getting away from that damn Luger as I unstrapped the ankle gun handing it over. The table between me and Reiner was too wide to use him as a shield. He started exploring the Colt running the barrel and dropping the bullets one by one onto the chess board.

"Our game Mr Kessler. Why don't we call it a draw?" Cackling with his shoulders at the edge of my eye, my head positioned stiff towards Kristof.

"The Colt's were always your weapon of choice. The American design is somewhat clunky but effective. The three inch barrel on the smaller model is an admiral innovation . . . a limited accuracy however. The function of the weapon is about accuracy Mr Kessler, would you agree."

"The Colt 13 is a handy weapon. Light and wearable. I can demonstrate it's accuracy Mr Reiner."

"That won't be necessary my friend." I was free to move my head as Reiner peered over his spectacles squinting with both eyes. "Do you remember me at all Mr Kessler?"

"I've had a few brandy's. However, if you mean maybe a run in on the battlefield . . . then yes. I can picture you in a German uniform."

Trying to chase my drink as I lifted my arm Kristof barked.

"STAY STILL KESSLER!"

"Fortunately I wasn't near the battlefield Mr Kessler. I was searching. Wondering if you had any entangled memory left from the old you."

"I can't recall you in any previous cases I've solved Mr Reiner. Unless you were the one that got away."

Grinning and standing from the chair, arms behind his back he stepped towards the fire. Kristof's glasses reflected the flame from the mirror, keeping the gun fixed in position. Reiner held both hands out and gathered the heat next to the surround while muttering to Kristof in what sounded German.

'He doesn't seem to recall.' I translated. If Kristof turns a blind eye, the kerosene lamp is inbound. If this place goes up in smoke then so be it. Still kicking myself over the chum I chewed in the chess game. They planned the whole thing. There's another Colt in the car so I better take it easy on the brandy.

"Mr Kessler." Reiner approached with a different countenance, trying to render a genuine smile.

"You were curious about my latest inventions. Now we can share the knowledge. Relax Mr Kessler, I won't be a moment."

His shoes treaded the stairwell while me and Kristof had our catch up. The dagger eyed stare of betrayal I fired from the back of my mind pierced his glasses. He knew, I was crouching at his door. One mistake and 'It's curtains for the old boy,' as the British used to say.

LIBRARY OF SOULS

"Please Mr Kessler. You will understand soon why it has to be this way. My intentions are not mendacious or the killing kind. We need your insight regarding the Terminal."

I had a wandering thought that maybe he was bluffing.

"I assume the Luger isn't loaded?"

"Your curiosity seems to have returned Mr Kessler. An admirable quality, one reason why we need your insight. However, the bullet will not be stopped if it leaves the barrel."

I heard many stories during the war about the butchers block so I'd prefer the bullet. Taking a chance I motioned my glass side to the side, signalling my eyes towards the drinks cabinet.

Steadfast with no expression he wasn't for turning so seconds later I leaned forward to stand.

"SIT DOWN."

BAAANG! He squeezed the trigger and the mirror to my side exploded inside out. Breaking violently into shards, the glass rained onto my shoulders as I drew my hands above my head. Crouched into the chair, my face buried in the arm, the final fragments descended onto the floor with a clatter. Carefully raising my head and blowing my shoulder Kristof wore a smile ear to ear. I had a croaked chuckle and Kristof followed, both of us amused. Reiner bounded down the stairs furnishing a Luger at arms length while I laid in wait for the turning of Kristof's head. He remained unmovable.

"Easy now Mr Kessler. I'm sorry for the interruption Mr Reiner. You could say we've broken the ice. I'm certain we have a clear understanding." Kristof asserted.

"You said he was a good shot Mr Reiner. Maybe it was the inaccuracy of the Luger?"

Reiner couldn't smile, only grin while he lowered his gun. His other hand brandished a menacing copper mask. A single chamber of round glass bonded at the centre with embellished layers of switches on the sides. I'd never seen anything of the kind. Lets hope it's still in the development phase I got to thinking. A blunted thud came from near the windows at the back of the room, echoing from inside the library. Then another deep thud from behind the door. My eyebrows raised but Kristof and Reiner didn't seem surprised by the sounds. Eye to eye I tried to elicit a reason and Kristof placed his index finger over his lips for me to be quiet, giving the order for Reiner to maintain guard while instructing me to hold out both hands together. He then proceeded to tie a wire around my wrists sealed with two knots.

"Comfortable Mr Kessler?"

"Of course. I'm used to being tied up in other peoples problems."

The library doors opened. A woman and a man appeared. They were covered in a black tar substance head to toe. I didn't know what it was. It wasn't clothing, more like an painted outfit shrink-wrapped onto their skin. They walked bare footed and each handed Kristof what looked like a wristwatch.

"Miss Taberna and Mr Wiseman are back from their appointment Mr Kessler." His satirical grin embellished an earlier intuition about the ‘we’ and ‘many’ he referred too. Kristof insisted they needed to bathe and rest. As the woman walked past she glanced at me.

“Good to have you back.” She remarked. Smiling and following the man towards the staircase I became confused while Reiner and Kristof procured an air of glee.

“Please Mr Kessler.” Kristof gestured towards the library. I slowly opened my legs and pushed my shoulders forward to stand. My hands touching the floor grabbing a shard of glass, I precariously edged towards the door. Over my shoulder Reiner smiled, gun in hand. Searching my thoughts for calm amidst the anxiety ‘The Perpetual Presence’ carved into the casing I stepped down into the library didn’t help. The clock chimed behind my ears conjuring a memory of the tolling of the bell. Is this the last room of my existence? I have to maintain my composure, the end game in chess has many opportunities.

Larger than the living quarters, I shuffled past a myriad of books, a grand piano and more unusual artefacts. Coaxing me onto a green leather couch, my hands tied, I got the impression Kristof was in his chariot. His stool pigeon Reiner sat stone faced at the end of the couch wielding the Luger.

"Our earlier conversation Mr Kessler about the Terminal. You might still be pondering on what it is, where it is and what does it do?" Kristof has guided this conversation all along, having me holding on to loose ends.

"Has it anything to do with the machines in the schoolhouse or the bodies missing on the lake? Maybe hogs running off the cliff or a mine collapse?"

"Consolidation always helps. Your prompts are not unreasonable so let us confirm that, the mine collapse has nothing to do with us."

"So what about the schoolhouse machines?" I asked Kristof.

He offered a small grin and placed his hand in his jacket pocket with a steely eyed glance at Reiner while nodding his head.

"It is a very long story Mr Kessler." Reiner muttered.

"You've got a captive audience, unless you want to brief me tomorrow."

Amused by my response, his grin thrived a devilish cackle shunting both shoulders. Only to return with a serious glum.

"To encapsulate your understanding Mr Kessler, what we had was a system called 'Cyclone Genesis' during the war. The machines we had built could house a body inside. Comfortability was not overlooked on the original designs. Unfortunately they weren't leather clad, but the synthetics were soft and had little complaints."

"The Sheriff had a different slant on barbarism."

"You elude to Mr Dalton. He is entitled to his own perspective. Any progress in a scientific field will always be susceptible to the margin of error. The Genesis effect could only be completed with crude technology and blue blood from an octopus. How you may ask? We would infuse the octopus hemocyanin into the bloodstream because it contains copper, rather than the human hemoglobin which contains iron. The copper was the conduit in the blood when connected to the generator - creating the cyclone through an electrical charged machine. The Genesis effect was the entry into the Terminal. In some strange way we have to thank your friend Sheriff Dalton for his hard work. The burning of the machines and the bodies. After all, we couldn't figure a way how to dispose of the old equipment." He cackled from the back of his throat with his lips closed while his head bobbed.

"How do you return from the Terminal?" I was buying time from Reiner while slowly biting at the wrist wire with the glass. Kristof proceeded to unlock a wooden cabinet near the piano.

"I detect a sense of fear Mr Kessler. Already you seek the antidote . . . one benefit is you cannot age or die once inside. Getting killed inside will respawn you in a random location. There are many seekers still trapped within the Griffin Terminal from years ago. However to answer your question, then yes, there is a way out."

"A victim trapped in purgatory, is that the margin of error within the progressive field?"

"You mean volunteer Mr Kessler. Volunteer, not victim."

"The copper mask - It's purpose Mr Reiner?"

Standing from the couch and sidestepping towards the library wall, keeping me at gun point, he placed the copper mask on a hook at head height. Then with a proud exhalation.

"A combination of function and form. An enigmatic creation that has taken me many,

many years to perfect." He pressed on the side of the mask as a light emanated from inside. A mechanical burr then whirring sound dropped to a snapping click. The same eerie noise from his room. Then, suddenly, it began to shape shift, the copper exterior locking into different positions. "This is your entry into the Terminal."

I was petrified of the mechanism, giving me more impetus to free my wrists. Keeping composed I laughed aloud at Reiner's face. Visibly annoyed at my disrespectful spout he calmed to a grinning smile with an aggressive nudge of the gun, returning to the couch. Nodding his head at the mask with a smirk.

"Fortunately for you, I have added a leather strap to the invention. This will make your journey more comfortable Mr Kessler."

My arms stayed in-between my legs while I continued to etch away at the wire on my wrists with the glass shard. The mask is frightening and damn ugly like Reiner. I need a way out.

"I assume the mask replaced the machines. So tell me, the victims inside the Terminal, how do you communicate?"

"Very good Mr Kessler, the old system is dead, correct." Visibly annoyed, his face scrunched centre as he breathed another sardonic laugh.

“Volunteers if you recall, not victims . . . Mr Kristof will explain and demonstrate how we operate. You’ve become a suckling baby after your spanning. We need to return you to solid food.”

A disengaging thought with his remark. I know who I am! Not gonna be long before I can relieve Reiner of his command and get the hell outa here. Kristof was busy preparing an object he wheeled out of the wooden cabinet. Standing from his knees at the back he unveiled another contraption. Three round panes of glass, pitch black but strangely reflective connected by a centre rod. My hands were nearly free.

“A fascinating device known as ‘The Looking Glass’ Mr Kessler. These are obsidian mirrors, each one made from volcanic rock and highly polished. This enables us to peer inside the node on the long wave form . . . what we call the Griffin Terminal.” He took the black wristwatch that Miss Taberna had given him and with a distinct click onto his wrist, stood to face the mirror. “Please stand, come closer. Let us marvel at pure potential, a world within a world Mr Kessler.”

The last thread of the wire was shredding as I kept rotating my wrists with the shard clenched at the end of my fist. Reiner stood and began gesturing the gun as I opened my legs, crouching forward to stand, realising my hands were finally free. Kristof's appearance began to change. A stiffening up of his body while his eyes switched to a bright white, they were emitting beams of light. His reflection through the mirrors of the looking glass spooked me as Reiner moved into view giving me a flash thought: 'I ain't going anywhere near his terminal' springing me into action.

"NEIN." Reiner bleated as I sidestepped him and wrapped the wire around the gun and his hand, pointing it towards Kristof's back. He jerked to pull up the gun with both our fingers on the trigger and shot 'BANG' into the roof beams. My hands gripped Reiner's wrist, elbowing him twice in the face with the third cracking his nose to a blood spatter. Kicking Kristof in the back propelled him into the mirrors as they split apart, head first he landed onto his contraption. Reiner's gun grip held strong as his teeth sunk into my shoulder punching my kidney from behind. Scuffling to direct the barrel at Kristof I yelled aloud to gun shots into the library walls as his eyeballs raged bloodshot. Another 'BANG' made the piano zimmer, then twisting the gun away from the trigger guard I snapped his finger bone. His vicious bite chewed deeper into my flesh making me howl. Tripping his leg to the floor into a wrestle, I gained the upper hand. My shoe stamped his wrists to bleed his grasp on the Luger and finally kneeling onto his blooded nose the gun was mine. I stood to order. "TO YOUR FEET." With the scruff of his hair I marched him over to the hanging mask with the steel barrel stoking the back of his head. "Take a good look Reiner. All that work is gonna be going up in smoke like a Viking funeral. You can wear the mask while I torch the ship." Kristof started to groan and snake on the floor.

"STAY STILL KRISTOF!" Turning his head to the side, mouth open and nose bleeding. His surprised appearance help rekindle my spirit. Now I could finally go home I thought. Bending Reiner's arm behind his back until he cried out I pushed him forward.

"Stay right there Kristof . . . disappointing it is, not being able to make the trip into the Terminal. I apologise for having to leave early. Maybe some friends from the bureau can visit and you can explain to them where it is and what it is?"

"You don't understand Kessler DAMN YOU! You've been part of this all along."

"You can't say I haven't tried to play ball Kristof." Nesting the barrel on the back of Reiner's head. I gripped his jacket, pulling him backwards towards the library opening. Firing a final shot into the side of the piano to hear the warped zinged zimmer of the strings. "On that note Kristof, I won't forget your impeccable service at the Lodge. I ain't a heavy tipper but I'll leave what I can on the plate. Maybe see you in the next life."

"SHAH MAT." A guns hammer cock clicked at the back of my skull. A female voice. "The King is dead remember Mr Kessler?" My hope dwindling, I considered squeezing the trigger knowing I couldn't become a prisoner again.

"Your not a prisoner Mr Kessler. You are one of us."

In that split second, my eyes closed, I journeyed through in my mind and pulled the trigger. The soft voice feeding back telling me I'm part of the team was my guardian angel on the ascension. My grip slackened around the gun butt. Then a huge 'SLAP' across my face followed by a bellowing punch into my stomach took me to my knees. I folded like a paper bag with my nose scraping the cold wooden floor. Then came a leather shoe into my gonads as my stomach rattled my tonsils and made me gawp silently like a helpless deer in the wild.

"That's ENOUGH Reiner." Kristof shouted.

"Du Narr, Kessler, du wirst sehen." Reiner growled as he lifted me under my arms and threw me head first onto the couch. I curled back into the foetus position, the pain was excruciating. My blurred vision made me want to hear that soft voice again over my shoulder.

"Get the aid kit Miss Biedermann quickly." It was Kristof's tone of voice I faintly heard while still out of phase. "Reiner sit him up and tie a strap around that shoulder. Stop it from bleeding out." The pain moved from my bowels to my upper arm as the adrenaline subsided and could fully open my eyes to witness the carnage. Reiner sat opposite, fashioning a splint for his finger while being daubed on his split nose by Miss Biedermann. It looked fully broken and a snigger quaffed from the side of my mouth. Enraged he made a bee line for me and Kristof shouted.

"NO REINER." I raised my palm for peace and realised my shoulder was shot at. He must have teeth like an animal I thought as my arm dropped limp. Miss Biedermann sat aside as I felt the whisky burn on the gaping bite wound then the tightening of the bandage wrapping across my chest. I grabbed the whisky bottle and toked a few heavy's looking at Reiner with a smile as he snarled with resentment. Kristof, while picking up his device pieces kept giving signals to Reiner almost in sign language, damn I thought, no more surprises. Patched up and still dizzy wanting my escape I rose to my feet only to have cold gun metal jabbed into my temple by Miss Biedermann.

"Please Mr Kessler. Less movements the better. Please be seated."

"Let us get back to being civilised now Mr Kessler. Just so you know, Miss Biedermann was an elite German sniper in the field of war. A hired assassin for the elite guard. We have crossed the first bridge. Now let us move onto the water and unravel your destiny." Kristof polished the mirrors, attaching them one by one to the centre pole while relaying his running dictum.

"There is a book within this library that belongs to you. As you have no previous knowledge of The Entanglement you volunteered to engage in, we need to take the necessary steps to re-educate your origins. None of us here have done this before as anyone who has soul spanned can always access the 'old you'." He looked at Miss Biedermann, then at Reiner and nodded. "It's time Mr Reiner . . . hand him the book."

Reiner traversed the library ladder to the squeak of brass castors inside the rail. Moving around ten feet to the left he leant over to take hold of a red book from the shelf. Stepping down he handed me a book. An emblem on the front with the characters A and S entangled - titled AlwaySeptember. The texture of the cover pulled and stretched, resembling skin. I opened the sleeve to turn the leafs with encoded characters, with many blank pages towards the back.

"These are not books Mr Kristof are they?" My mouth dried of moisture from anxiety and confusion. "Tell me, what am I witnessing here? Is it some kind of codex and for what purpose?"

"Codex isn't a false assumption. This might seem absurd to the sharpest of intellect . . . or to a seeker a blessing in disguise. You are the latter, just like ones before you. This library of books are living profiles, seekers inside the Griffin Terminal. They are active as we speak, each one has soul spanned and become part of The Entanglement. The owner is the only one partaking in their writings, until all the parts are written. You are the only one able to read your own book . . . your own soul." He sauntered closer, Reiner sitting stone cold across pointing his pistol while Biedermann shifted back into the corner of the couch.

"Can you understand the encoded characters within your book Mr Kessler? Please take your time, have another look."

I opened the book again and perused the pages. Staring intensely an aberration, this cannot be. Suddenly the characters slowly shifted around into a readable dialect. Letters became words, then sentences, then paragraphs and what appeared to be directions. Astonished to what I was witnessing I kept a brazen face, looking confused. Turning the leafs more quickly then flicking through the blanks, closing on the back cover.

"It makes no sense at all. Are you sure it is my book?"

"He's lying DAMN YOU!" Reiner shouted.

"Mr Reiner, please be patient. Take your time Mr Kessler. Stare long and hard at the pages to see if they come to life."

I did the second round and played their bluff. I guess this is why they needed me. There must be something in the book. I stared and witnessed the characters moving slowly then snapping into coherence. I kept my poker face firm for a few minutes until I closed the book with both hands.

"Please Mr Kristof this is not a language I recognise. What am I supposed to be seeing within the scrambled characters?"

"He's lying Mr Kristof. He can clearly see what it says." Reiner spouted.

"Please Mr Reiner. Maybe his entanglement cannot engage because your teeth are still in his shoulder. Take your time Mr Kessler, relax. You might need a recap to recall the old you." Kristof pulled a chair at the side of me out of the line of fire. His ostensible smile coaxing my game.

It soon became clear I was in a deeper riddle than I thought. Stripping back the thoughts I peered into the void what I thought was me. Running through my head I kept refusing to accept the divergent teachings. To reconcile I am somewhere inside someone else's body cannot be so.

"Tell me . . . Who am I?"

"Your real name is an acronym of Always September, the book you hold. Tayler Ewambes.

Your original soul. You were a detective who came to investigate a homicide a few years back. An inquisitive mind that volunteered to venture into the Terminal."

"That's impossible. I have no recollection of a man named Tayler. Yes, I'm a detective Mr Kristof but there are many detectives." He could see I wasn't buying into the rhetoric and sighed while adjusting his spectacles.

"You had another agent you invited to the Lodge, his name was Dan Kessler. It is here we finally arrive at your current situation. Yes, I can see your puzzling highbrow. Please allow me to explain."

I was dumbstruck with a chill down my spine. A torn shoulder pinched me as I moved, grabbing my bicep to ease the pain. I searched Miss Biedermann's eyes for comfort or consolidation of what was being relayed. Pensive I lifted my head to Kristof with a nod to hear his version of events.

"We have waiting patiently three years on your return. Knowing of your arrival because you appeared in the Looking Glass. The transportation you underwent is called soul spanning. Your encoded profile is written in your book, the very essence of 'you' in the aether, known as the 'Akasha'. The millions of magnetite crystals in your brain are tethered to the aether, this is how consciousness works. The powerful cache inside the magnets is what we tap into to soul span to another host . . . once entangled you can continue to span effectively if you so wish, to become immortal as a mortal. Your still a product of time though Mr Kessler."

"I won't have my beliefs shoe horned that easily Mr Kristof. Are you suggesting . . . that . . . that I entangled . . . or spanned into."

"Yes. You are still a detective if that's any consolation. Agent Kessler was in the war, however you were never there Tayler. Something altered with your entanglement, but we know you are still 'encoded' within Agent Kessler's body as crude as that may sound. I deplore prevarication, however it is true."

"So where's the old me? Tayler Ewambes? Where's my body?"

"Buried in the woods." Kristof said.

"I buried you Kessler, and I don't mind doing it again." Reiner cackled while squinting in pain, his nose bleeding through the bandages.

Kristof's glee paraded the Looking Glass object, pacing front to back touching the glass edges.

"You see Mr Kessler with a few changes to the present, the future is all but assured. The gentleman who drove the initial experiment, Samual Alderman was able to soul span many times . . . from one destiny to the next, tied as a knot in time each span. He mapped a large percentage of the Griffin Terminal to find many gates, the discovery of the Lion's Gate, it's existence, it's potential. It was the former you, Detective Tayler, who came close to finding the key to that gate. The co-ordinates are written down in your book from the many times you ventured inside as the 'old you'.

"What do you mean? I've been inside the Terminal before?

"Yes, many times. It will be Always September for you Tayler. A deciduous reinvention of the former you, your season of change . . . your spanning into Kessler and your time in the Terminal." He lifted his chair back near the piano and picked up the copper mask hanging from a hook on the library shelf. Asking Reiner to place his gun down and insisting he stand adjacent. He then started fixing the mask onto Reiner's face, bracing the leather strap around the back of his head.

"So how do I . . . how do I get the 'old me' back?"

"You cannot go back, the perpetual presence is our existence, now . . . or in the future. Are you still wanting to indulge in the illusion of free will Kessler? His hand twisting the levers on the masks surface made it gleam. A whirring followed by a burr winding to a snapping click. Then began a mechanical clunking as the copper started overlapping, shape shifting on Reiner's face. The single glass portal shone bright from the inside. Kristof then reached out and connected a light bulb with blue liquid into the back of the copper mask. The bulb began to illuminate as he communicated something in German close to his ear. Holding Reiner's forearm he turned towards me. "There is a distinct possibility you can find the 'old you' inside the Terminal . . . your memory could return, a plausibility."

"Get me in there Kristof. I wanna meet the 'old me'.

"Very well but you have to commit to wanting to go - it is not a flippant decision. What about your detective work Mr Kessler?"

His satire never fades. I'm still not convinced about his proposition although beguiled of his theories. I am the real me. Detective Tayler seems more like an old friend of theirs and I'm here through coincidence. I brushed my hand over the AS characters on the front of the book in my lap. The phenomenon of the changing characters within the pages hmmm . . . an illusion maybe. Regardless, I need to hatch a new plan. Biedermann, still the stalwart as we met eye to eye, the gun barrel on point. The mask mechanism was becoming louder and brighter.

"My detective work is my work Kristof."

"The place where I take you Kessler is not governed by mans laws. How would you cope without the necessary parameters?"

"I trenched with a machine gun on foreign soil with no ticket home."

"Well I guess the 'new you' has a tougher approach which will no doubt help you on your journey." Kristof gave over the liquid blue luminous bulb while he stepped aside. Pulsing light flashed more frequent as mechanical movements on the copper mask began fusing, overlapping faster and faster. Louder became the clunking of the metal collisions as Reiner started to shake profusely. The bright light inside the glass portal concentrated into a beam, hitting the wall behind me. Astonished and fascinated was I as the observer. Kristof, encapsulated in the moment with an artful glee held his hands wide open. “Now Kessler you can witness the entrance into the long wave. His materialisation into the Griffin Terminal.”

GRIFFIN TERMINAL

As Reiner juddered behind the luminous haze a smokey black cloud emerged from behind his head. Slowly but surely engulfing his entirety and swallowing the radiated light. A centred flash appeared, then, like smoke in a hurricane - he was gone. The copper mask dropped to the floor as the sound of a crashing cymbal. An eerie silence ensued as the black cloud dissipated. I crouched forward, my mouth unfurled in disbelief edging to stand. Kristof waved to Biedermann to lower the gun as I searched for contemplation in his eyes.

"Please Kessler . . . as you will."

Shuffling precariously towards the mask laying on the floor. Waving my hands through the last whispers of the decaying cloud. Crouching with reticence over the touch of my flesh on the copper. Poor Reiner I thought, it must have been as hot as a smokehouse in there.

"There is no heat - it is a cold fusion process." Kristof observed my reservation of handling the mask. Taking hold and flipping it over, it appeared unscathed. I swiped my feet from side to side around where Reiner was standing, looking up, then down. With an overwhelming incoherence, I asked, what was I experiencing? Unless this is another illusion! I calmed my composure surrounded by a foreboding anxiety of my own fate. Staring into the portal as the copper reflected the shimmer of the wall lights, I found humour.

"Well . . . at least there won't be a drain on your electric now Reiner's gone. Shame, I was just getting to know him." A reflection entered the glass as I felt the butt of a gun on the back of my head sinking me into the ocean depths. Didn't see that one coming. I'd like to think Biedermann was only executing Kristof's plans because she had too. I started to open bleary eyed to the flush of smelling salts, trying to touch my face made me start yanking at ties on my wrists around the chair arms.

"DAMN YOU KRISTOF!"

"I apologise in advance Kessler. I was wondering of a last request while you were sleeping. The curious can make home to assumptions, which made me prepare a double brandy for you." Placing the brandy glass on the side table he wheeled the obsidian mirrors closer. "You are a seeker, a player or a creator at any point in time. Now I need you to be all three when you step inside the Terminal Kessler. There are many unfriendly seekers lurking who need a way out so it's imperative you listen to the instructions I communicate. You will be able to hear me telepathically, that is, we will be connected through this device. Similar to a watch for your wrist with my specific frequency on. This is your only way out remember." He opened his hand as Miss Biedermann placed a black watch into his palm with a pulsing light in the middle.

"So I have you constantly in my head Kristof? That's great."

He clicked the watch device on the back, fitting tightly around my wrist. The pulsing made my vision clearer, my reflection in the mirror made me aware of my eyes radiating white light. Biedermann's eyes also were illuminating and the final snap of the wristwatch onto Kristof.

"You'll need it to navigate inside the Terminal. From my position I have your eyes through the Looking Glass to guide us. We have lost thousands of seekers before you."

"What's happened to the lost ones? Where did they go?"

"It's an opened ended question. I'm afraid I don't have the answer. We can only assume they entered a gate to be released back into this world. Their books in the library have stopped writing codec. Remember you cannot die inside the Terminal, it's a node on the long waveform, it can't be broken, only altered."

"So their journey into the Terminal wasn't successful."

"Success is the pursuit of a worthy idea Kessler. Human optimism is a super power." Damn you Kessler flashed into my thoughts. Searching for some hopeful humanity from him was a needle in a haystack. I mean, where the hell did Reiner end up?

"Tell me. What is the Lion's Gate?" Tipping blue liquid into the bulb, preparing my eventuality he pointed his finger upwards into the air.

"A saviour to mankind's most frightening question . . . Death."

"I hit death head on most days Kristof. Is that what your afraid of?"

"We are sentient beings my dear Kessler. Creatures that can suffer and feel pain, the power to perceive, reason and think. Death is incalculable, it arrives at any moment. Pursuing an alternative to death seems a worthwhile journey."

"What happened to Samual Alderman, the man behind the curtain who spanned other individuals bodies?"

"Eventually he opened a gate to the animal kingdom, inadvertently soul spanning into a creature. Unfortunately there is no return from that gate, so we avoid still to this day."

"Wow the animal kingdom. So what became of Alderman?"

"I cannot answer that." Following Kristof's eyes towards Miss Biedermann as he ran his fingers down the side of the mirrors on the Looking Glass. "Although I believe in destiny, I often question its existence based on the happenings of Samuel Alderman. As for yourself, you seem to be stalling your own fate. Stop waiting for your destiny to expire Kessler."

Clasping the tabled glass to my side . . . "Would you care for your brandy now?"

With limiting choice my humbling lips touched the edge of the glass. Flushing the warm liquor to a satisfying breath I held out for one more question.

"Tell me, how do you soul span?" He grinned at Biedermann with a nod as my vision darkened feeling the weight of the mask being pushed onto my face. The crease of the leather strap behind my head tightening as my gleaming white eyes lit the portal housing from inside. Kristof tapped on the glass with his knuckle.

"There is a method to soul spanning. However, now you have a date with destiny Kessler. Once the magnetite in your head fuses with the copper in the octopus blood you will materialise into the black void. You will be dragged towards the light, a vortex, then spat out of the sky into the Griffin Terminal. A black goo morphs your skin from the void, so be aware, ripping this from your face when you land will allow you to breathe." Clasping the blue bulb he began to fix a tube to the back of my head. At this point I tingled with anxiety, especially witnessing Reiner's shaky exit. "Your journey will embark in less than three minutes Kessler -

Reiner is inside waiting and Miss Biedermann will follow your entry, guarding you from any hostility. Your safety is paramount, we need you back here to interpret co-ordinates within your book. Hopefully the trip will germinate your memory."

"Good to know your looking out for me Kristof."

"My pleasure Kessler. I'm excited to be fracking your dormant potential."

He tapped on the side of my face activating the mask. A sounding of the burr registered the whirring mechanism. That inevitable wind down to a definitive click. The colliding of the copper metallic, the shape shifting gained momentum. Intense clunking louder and louder in my ears. Placing the glowing bulb in a housing at the chair side Kristof moved a few paces back. His grin barely visible through the portal as the rush of the cold blood washed the back of my hcad. My arms and legs started to uncontrollably shake. The chair legs and my shoes clattered the floor then the eerie smoky cloud enveloped the lens. My vision zero, my eyes stinging from the bright light, my ears burning with the noise. I bellowed out an angry roar that echoed . . . once, twice, then to a reverberated feedback of my existence. The shaking had stopped, the clunking of metal turned to a ringing silence. Finally, an awakening within the transitory black void.

Suspended I was somehow. A weightlessness, a foreboding apprehension within a huge lake, floating with no sound. The darkness resembled black velvet. Was it a vast space or a small box my encapsulation? I raised my hand for register but still, no vision. A light, a tiny glint in the distance. Was I moving? Was it me approaching the pin hole or the light moving towards me? My helpless cessation drawing nearer to the light caused my eyes to widen, I observed movement. Squinting at the inevitable, a violent motion within the light source was clearly swirling at tremendous speed. A stark realisation of the end of my protraction - an inauguration through the vortex.

#_#

#_#

Kessler?

##_ ## Kessler check in

#_#

#_#

Kessler?

#_#

##_ ## Kessler. Can you hear me?

#_#

IM HERE. Inside the Terminal.

##_ ## I'm at the forest's edge.

#_#

Stay there for a moment and listen for any signs.

Emerging from the cold soil at a forest's edge, engulfed in black gel, I was overwhelmed with anomaly. A vast landscape cut with blackened trees and mountainous terrain. The sky's shade of colours were mixing, converging into shapes like softly blown blankets. My skin bore a likeness to rubber, as I touched, covered head to toe in the tar substance. In the distance, a sound. I couldn't gauge the direction. It isn't clear. Wait . . . over there.

#_#

Kristof - how do I know the sound of another seeker?

What can you hear?

#_#

Sounds like a Ravens croak.

Move in that direction Kessler. RUN!

Roger that.

The sprint confused my senses, the ground thickets had no effect on my bare feet. I picked up pace, my speed was abnormally fast. There it sounded again, the ravens call, northwest to my position. Gathering momentum through the forest's massive trees, hurtling forward with what felt like a motorcycle ride. My vision was acute.

#_#

Kristof what is the ravens call?

A seeker or a hunter you will find. They will have different eyes, like you.

I'm getting closer . . .

My advancement wasn't hindered through the forest's undergrowth, another rush, another dynamic force, a startling uniform motion. The blurry flickering of light through the trees caught my attention - whatever it was it was moving as fast as me. The calling of the raven was in the lights direction. I veered my trajectory, rallying closer until another croak echoed earshot. 'Stop' I thought, slowing rapidly to the snap of bush thickets and rustling of leaves. My legs crashed into the silent landscape with a heightened sensual perception. Out from the woodland there, standing as I am, another mans form. Eyes wide open, as bright as sunlight.

“What is your purpose?” His deep toned voice echoed as he stretched his arm pointing at my chest.

“I’m here to find the Lions Gate.” I responded while he circled around me in a speedy blur with his head moving up and down. I felt powerless.

“We are all here for the Lions Gate what say you?”

#_#

Kristof are you there? Kristof can you hear me?

#_#

Yes Kessler I’m here. Tell him you have the key to the seventh gate. The seventh part of the eschaton.

KONRAD MCLEAN

AUTHOR

Language is magic to inspire others. I'm eager to share more captivating stories with the world. We are all living colours in our seasons of change.

info@alwayseptember.com

www.alwayseptember.com

Published by Konaga Publishing Lancashire UK

Printed in Great Britain
by Amazon

46540525R00098